THE DREAM CATCHER

Hecate's Rebellion Book 4

Jade Hayes

TCA Publishing LLC

PROLOGUE

Leo Devereaux came awake with a start. His eyes traveled over the bedroom in search of what pulled him from sleep. Wind rattled the window in its frame and buffeted the house.

What the hell?

He sat up, frowning. The forecast for the night was calm, clear weather. He shouldn't be hearing anything but the soft sound of Keira breathing as she slept.

The window rattled again, harder, and the roar grew.

A glance at his wife revealed she was still asleep.

Quietly, so as not to wake her, he got out of bed and crept to the window to look out. Looking through the glass, the stars glowed in the night sky, but the barren tree branches waved in the wind. Dust, grass, and leaves swirled in the yard, lifting up into the dark sky.

As the cloud of debris coalesced, a feeling of dread filled Leo's gut. He had seen this before.

Watching silently, he waited, hoping he was wrong about what was coming, but knowing he wasn't. The debris swirled in an ever-tightening column, lifting higher until it surpassed the tree tops. The wind reached a fevered pitch, then the mass of swirling debris collapsed to the ground in a violent rush, scattering the leaves across the yard. A man and woman emerged from the dust, their tall forms moving with an elegance and grace toward the house.

"Well, fuck."

Turning away from the window, he strode back to the bed and shook Keira awake.

She grumbled at him and swatted at his hand.

"*Chère*, wake up. We've got company."

Her eyes fluttered open. "What?"

He threw her robe at her. "Put that on and your slippers and meet me downstairs."

"Leo, what's going on?"

"Hades is here."

She jackknifed, the air around her crackling with her anger, and her eyes took on a slight silver glow. "Goddammit. What the hell does he want? I swear, if he tries to take your soul again, I'm going to smite him where he stands." She shoved off the covers and stood. Leo's eyes drifted to her belly and the tiny life growing there, reminding him they had a lot more at stake now.

One corner of his mouth quirked as he pulled on a pair of jeans and stuffed his feet into some shoes. His fierce kitten. "Considering I'm his equal now, he'll have a hell of a fight on his hands from me first. I'm going to wake Ty and Penny."

She nodded, hopping slightly as she wiggled her foot into her slipper while trying to thrust her arms into the sleeves of her robe.

Striding down the hall, Leo stopped in front of Ty and Penny's bedroom. He rapped on the door before turning the knob and throwing it open.

Ty jerked awake. Blue flames licked brightly in his eyes before he realized who had intruded into his bedroom.

"Leo. What the hell?"

Penny stirred beside him. "What's going on?"

"Hades just landed outside. He brought Persephone with him."

Ty's epithet matched Leo's. Tossing the covers aside, he climbed out of bed and pulled a pair of athletic shorts out of the dresser.

"What the hell does he want now?"

Leo shrugged. Ty's guess was as good as his.

A loud pounding sounded through the house as Hades banged on the front door.

"Guess we're going to find out. I'll meet you downstairs." Spinning on his heel, he caught Keira's hand in his as she burst out of their bedroom, and ran down the hall. Together, they hurried down the stairs. The Christmas lights wrapped around the railing lit their way.

Hades banged again.

"Humans! Open the door."

Leo rolled his eyes. Even after all they did for the bastard, he still spoke to them like they were dirt beneath his boots.

The sound of Ty's heavy footfalls on the stairs had Leo striding forward to open the front door.

What he saw on the other side had him biting back the scathing rebuke on the tip of his tongue. Hades's hair was disheveled and his clothes rumpled, while Persephone looked as though she had been crying.

"May we come in?" Hades asked, his voice tired.

Hesitating only a moment, Leo nodded and stepped back.

Penny flipped on the lights and led them all into the living room.

Ty motioned for the gods to sit.

Like someone pulled the stuffing out of her, Persephone sank onto the sofa. Hades perched on the edge next to her, wringing his hands.

Alarmed, Leo sat in the chair adjacent to them. Something was very wrong.

Keira, Penny, and Ty settled onto the other sofa, opposite Hades and Persephone.

Leo shared a look with Ty, who had the same concerned expression on his face.

"What's going on? Why are you banging on my door at three a.m.?" Ty demanded.

Hades glanced at his wife, who poked him in the arm and nodded, glancing at them.

Running a hand through his hair, the god sighed. Leaning an arm on his thigh, his mouth flattened distastefully before he spoke.

"We need your help."

"Why?" Leo asked. "I thought we were just a pack of humans."

Hades smiled ruefully. "You are. But you're a useful pack of humans."

Persephone punched him in the arm. "Not helping."

Holding his hands up in supplication, Hades huffed out a breath. "Okay. Sorry." He sucked in a deep breath and continued. "It seems Hecate had a longer reach than I originally thought. Before the four of you captured her and brought her to me, she launched another plan. A backup, of sorts."

Dread pooled in Leo's stomach. "What kind of plan?"

"She set Phobos and Deimos loose on Earth."

"Who now?" Ty asked.

"Phobos and Deimos. They're Ares's twin sons. Fear and dread. They induce panic wherever they go. Those riots in Turkey and Greece earlier this month? That was them."

"Okay. Why do you look so upset? You're not exactly in love with the human race."

He looked at Persephone and took her hand. "Lately, I noticed a decline in the number of souls coming through my gate. Figuring they were going somewhere, I went to see our daughter, Melinoe, the goddess of spirits, to ask if she noticed an uptick in the number of ghosts roaming Earth. When I reached her home, no one was there, and it looked like there had been a struggle. We searched for her, but—"

He took a shaky breath. Tears welled in Persephone's eyes.

"We found her in some sort of strange stasis in the forests outside Hecate's compound." Blinking furiously, he continued. "I confronted Hecate, and she admitted she put plans in place as a backup should she get caught. She wouldn't say what all she had done, but I managed to uncover that Phobos and Deimos, at her request, somehow split Melinoe's body from her soul. I've scoured the underworld for her soul, but can't find it. I fear if we don't reunite it with her body soon, she will die forever. Hecate wanted to hurt me and knew the only way to do that was through my family."

Leo closed his eyes briefly. He didn't want to feel for Hades, but he did. If something ever happened to the baby Keira carried, it would utterly devastate him. "I'm sorry, Hades. How is it possible that she could die, though? I mean, she's immortal, like you, right?"

"Any god can be killed under the right circumstances. From what we can figure, they frightened her so much it caused the split. But until we—" he broke off and cleared his throat. "Until we find her soul, we won't know for sure."

Persephone sucked in a breath and stood, pacing to the window.

Leo watched her for a moment before turning back to Hades. "Do you know what they're planning, then? Or was it just to hurt you?" Leo asked, switching gears.

"Hecate refused to tell me anything, so I sent out a scout to track them and find out what they were up to. I couldn't find their location, but I learned that they have enlisted the help of a mortal man,

Brandon Henley, a descendant of Hypnos. The man is a psychiatrist, specializing in hypnotic treatment for mental disorders."

Ty's curse was loud and long. "That's awesome. So, we have a doctor—who basically messes with people's minds—with supernatural abilities. And here I thought we were unique."

Hades pointed at Leo. "*He* is unique. The rest of you are just three of many others with divine blood running through your veins. You have just unlocked your abilities. Many people don't even know they have them. Or, what they do have is just a heightened version of something normal, like speed, or a genius IQ. There are very, very few of you who know what you actually are."

Leo frowned at that, but pushed it to the back of his mind to contemplate at a later date. "Okay. So, if Henley's working with Phobos and Deimos, I take it he's inducing panic in his patients?"

Hades's nod was short and succinct.

"I fail to see how this requires our attention. I mean, I get you want them caught so they can face punishment for what they did to your daughter, but are they really an imminent threat to mankind? Seriously, how many people can Henley hypnotize at once?"

"And why us again?" Penny asked. "We fulfilled the prophecy we were part of."

Hades shook his head. "Given the right platform, he could hypnotize quite a few people. And it wouldn't be normal hypnosis. He'll have a greater influence on people's minds. Theoretically, he could make anyone do whatever he wished. As for why I—need the four of you, you'll have to take that up with the Oracle. When this new development occurred, I went to her and asked if this was a legitimate threat. She said yes, and that I needed you again." He shrugged. "I don't argue with the Oracle. That's Zeus's thing. I've learned I never win. So, here I am. Asking for help." The last part came through gritted teeth.

Leo rubbed his temples. "That's just fucking fantastic. You realize Keira's pregnant, right? I'm not willing to put her in the line of fire. I didn't want to the last time, but with the life of our child on the line, you can forget it. And even from behind the scenes, I don't know how much help she'll be. The pregnancy is screwing with her abilities."

Hades's expression turned grim. "I'm afraid you may not have much of a choice. The twins will likely bring the fight to you. After what happened this past summer, they know you four are the only ones on Earth who can stop them."

Pushing to his feet, Leo paced to the window to stare out at the still night.

"You won't be alone, though, this time," Hades continued.

Leo glanced back. "What do you mean?"

"The Oracle mentioned the four of you and *some of your friends*. I don't know who they are, but I think one of them is Dr. Henley's associate, Dr. Clary Moncrief. You need to go get Dr. Moncrief and bring her here. She is in grave danger. She has figured out that Dr. Henley is up to no good. My scout saw her fleeing their research facility yesterday afternoon. She was apparently quite terrified."

Keira immediately stood. "I'll go get my scrying materials."

Leo held out a hand. "*Chère*, hang on a second." He hated the idea they didn't have a choice in this, but he wanted to make sure they were all on the same page before jumping into the fire.

He motioned the others toward the door and looked at Hades. "Give us a minute."

Leading the others out of the room, he headed for the foyer in hopes they could talk privately. They stopped at the base of the staircase.

"Are we seriously considering partnering with the devil again?" Ty asked, his voice low.

"I don't think we have a choice," Keira said. "If what he says is true, mankind is in trouble—big trouble—if we don't."

"Are you sure you can do what needs to be done?" Leo asked. "Your abilities haven't exactly been reliable lately."

Keira ran a hand over the slight swell of her stomach. Leo's heart clenched with a deep and fierce love, just like it did every time he thought of the life growing inside of her. Her pregnancy hadn't been planned, but it definitely wasn't unwelcome. He couldn't wait to meet their child.

"Even with the havoc this child has wreaked on my abilities, I still think I need to try. What kind of world will we be bringing this little one into if I don't? Will there even be a world to bring him into? The way Hades talked, we could be facing a global war."

Leo pursed his lips, not pleased with this turn of events. Putting his pregnant wife in the middle of a fight amongst the Greek gods was not something he was keen on. But she was right. If they didn't help Hades, their child would be born into chaos.

"All right, but you're staying out of the action. Something goes down, you are getting locked in the bunker." After what happened over the summer, Ty had a safe room installed in the house that was damn near physically impenetrable. Keira warded it to make it magically impenetrable. Leo was adding one to their house in Louisiana as well. He wasn't about to leave his family vulnerable. Not now that he knew what hidden evils there really were in the world.

Keira narrowed her eyes at him, not liking being told what to do. "If I'm not needed, I will gladly stay out of the way."

Leo arched a brow. "Even if you are, you're going to stay out of it. I'll rig up something in the bunker so you can still be involved, but from a safe distance."

She bit the inside of her cheek, but nodded.

He eyed her warily, not sure if she had acquiesced because she agreed with him or because she was trying to placate him. It never boded well for him when she capitulated so easily.

"So, are we doing this, then?" Ty asked, breaking into Leo's thoughts.

Keira nodded before Leo could open his mouth. "Yes. I don't want to give birth to this child, only to bring him up in a war zone."

Leo didn't either.

"So, who are these friends he's talking about? Colin is the only one who knows about what we really are," Ty said, mentioning his partner.

Leo shrugged. "I'd say that's certainly possible. He did help some with Hecate."

Ty nodded. "Let's go tell Hades, then I'll call Colin and have him come over."

"I'll go get my scrying stuff." Keira scampered up the stairs to her magic room.

Re-entering the living room, Leo, Ty, and Penny stood shoulder to shoulder and faced the powerful deities who had come asking for their help. Persephone still looked utterly miserable, while Hades just looked exhausted. Leo couldn't help but think how human they looked at that moment.

He quickly shut down that line of thinking. They were far from human, and it would do him well to remember that.

Taking a deep breath, he stared straight at Hades. "We'll help."

CHAPTER 1

Twenty-four hours earlier...

Edges of her vision fuzzy, Clary Moncrief knew she was in a dream. Besides, nothing in the real world looked this strange. Golden grass waved in the warm breeze, tinged with the scent of the ocean. Thin clouds floated overhead in the bright sky. What made it strange, though, was the orange glow to everything. In the distance, the glow was stronger. It boiled up from the black clouds billowing over the mountains rising at the edge of the field where she stood. In the opposite direction, a tall stone wall ran as far as she could see, a sheer rock face behind it. Perhaps the strangest thing, though, was the enormous black castle perched atop a hill on the other side of the field. Its pointy turrets stood sentry over the world in which she stood.

Clary turned away from the castle and let her eyes rove the field. There was a peace here unlike any she'd ever experienced. Her entire being felt at rest. She closed her eyes and took a deep breath, savoring the feeling. She liked dreams like this. Clary often had lucid dreams, but they weren't always pleasant. Many times, she came awake in a dream to screams of terror or monsters. So far, other than the strange setting, this one was peaceful.

She opened her eyes and immediately took back her thought. Instead of the field, she now stood in a dark forest. Branches creaked overhead in the blustery wind. A shiver went down her spine as the chilly breeze blew over her. Goosebumps erupted on her arms, and she hugged herself to stay warm. Why couldn't her mind ever dress her right when it put her in these places? Would it be too much to conjure a sweatshirt?

Doing her best to ignore the cold, she walked forward, deeper into the creepy forest. Something crashed to the ground to her right. Clary shrieked and turned, eyes straining in the low light to see what made the noise. It didn't sound like a tree. More like something crashing through them. She backed away, only to hear the same noise behind her.

Okay, this one's weird, even for me. Clary tried to force herself to wake, closing her eyes and focusing on her bedroom, but it didn't work. Heart racing and a little unsure what was happening—she could always wake herself when things got hairy—she ran. She didn't know where she was going, but she knew she wanted away from here. She cast a glance at the sky, hoping to see a hint of the pretty sky where she first appeared. It seemed lighter to her left, so she took off toward it, praying she was right.

With her eyes trained on everywhere but forward, she nearly ran into the woman standing in her path. Clary yelped and skidded to a stop. She lost her balance and landed in a heap on the forest floor. Crunchy leaves and damp dirt shifted beneath her hands as she scrambled back to her feet.

Upright, she looked at the woman before her, and her eyes widened. She didn't know what she was, but she wasn't human. Her body was two-toned. The left side was as black as the darkest ink, right down to the tips of her hair. Her right was whiter than the whitest snow. In the low light, that side glowed, while her left side almost disappeared into the darkness. She wore a simple, sleeveless white dress. The skirt billowed around her ankles. As Clary stared at her, she realized the woman wasn't standing on the ground. She hovered just above it.

A scream bubbled up her throat, but she swallowed it, not knowing how it would make this creature react. Instead, she held her ground and stared into the woman's glowing amber eyes.

"Help me."

Clary's eyes bounced around the forest, looking for the source of the voice. The woman's lips never moved.

"Help me." The woman held out a hand.

She stared at it. There was no way she was taking this thing's hand. "Why do you need my help?"

"Because I'm lost. And they're chasing me."

"Chasing you? Who's chasing you?"

More crashes sounded from behind the woman. A wailing echoed through the trees.

"You must help me, Clary Moncrief." The woman's image began to fade.

"Wait!" Clary stepped forward, hand outstretched. "How do I help you? Who are you running from? What's your name?"

"Help me." The woman faded away, leaving Clary standing amongst the trees.

"Dammit!" She spun a full circle, but saw nothing but dark forest. Freaked out and angry, Clary closed her eyes and tried to force herself awake again. This time, it worked, and she woke in her bed, sweating.

She sat up and shoved away the blankets, swinging her legs out of bed to plant her feet on the rug. She dug her toes into the plush carpet, trying to ground herself in reality.

"What the hell was that?" Her long blonde hair fell forward as she leaned her elbows on her knees. She pushed it out of her face, then stood in need of some water. That had to be one of the strangest dreams she'd ever had. And she'd had some doozies.

As she walked downstairs to get a glass of water, she tried to shake the images of the ghostly apparition from her mind. How her brain conjured up such a thing, she didn't know. She must have seen an actress made up like that on a TV show or a movie and didn't remember.

All she knew was going back to sleep would not be easy.

CHAPTER 2

Heels clacking on the tile hallway floor, Clary turned the corner into her research partner, Dr. Brandon Henley's office. She was tired of waiting for the data from their latest round of sleep study patients. She knew he had it. She asked him about it this morning. He told her he'd get it to her once he reviewed it all. It had already been a week. It didn't take that long to read it. Especially when he'd been the one conducting most of the study. She just wanted the sections on REM sleep. The last group saw a marked reduction in REM and an increase in deep sleep, but they still complained their level of fatigue didn't change.

She ran her eyes over the pile of papers and folders on his desk and sighed. His office didn't look any better than hers. For brilliant people, they could both use better organizational skills. She walked around and sat in his chair, pulling the first stack toward her. Lucky for her, she found what she needed right away. Clary flipped open the folder and scanned it. A frown formed between her eyebrows. What the hell was this? She read further, her eyes widening with each word.

This couldn't be right. She set the file down and rubbed her eyes, then blinked hard. Maybe her sleep-deprived brain wasn't seeing it right. She picked it up again and read the page once more. Shock rippled through her as the words didn't change.

She glanced up, her gaze going to the window that showed the hallway. He could come back at any minute, and she doubted he wanted her reading this. Flipping through the pages again, anger burned hot in her belly. Eyebrows furrowed, she stared hard at the papers. What the hell was he thinking even attempting something like this? How did she not know he'd gone off on this tangent? It certainly explained why her patients kept complaining they were so tired, even after a full night's sleep. They weren't getting a full night's sleep. They were up, moving around, and performing strange tasks. He'd been sending her altered data.

Clary glanced at the door again, then turned back to the file, reading more, hoping to find out why—and how—he was hypnotizing their patients to perform increasingly violent tasks on lab animals. At the end of the file, attached to the back of the last page, she found a series of sticky notes covered in Brandon's handwriting. Her eyes widened as she read each one. Words like war and global chaos jumped out at her. From what she could tell, he wanted to hypnotize people to become ruthless soldiers.

Alarmed, she scraped the file back together, then reached for the computer mouse and gave it a quick shake to wake up the monitor. She needed to see if he had any electronic files on this project. To see how far he had gone. If she could even get in. Their computers were password-protected, and she didn't know Brandon's passcode.

The screen jumped to life, taking her straight to his desktop. He hadn't bothered to log out before he left his office. With another quick glance through the window, she opened his hard drive and started scanning the file names. Nothing popped out at her she didn't recognize.

She quickly clicked through his hard drive, checking in a couple other locations, but still found nothing.

Satisfied that there was nothing on this computer, she quickly put it back to sleep.

Her eyes landed on the folder with the hypnosis research. She bit her lip, looking around the room. Her heart thundered in her ears as she contemplated her next move.

She couldn't leave this here and risk him leaving with it. It was evidence. But if she took it, he *would* come after her. Brandon would not want this to get out. Not only would the authorities come after him, but it would thwart his plans. She still wasn't sure how he got people to do the things he did, but she couldn't allow him to continue to do so. And he would, of that she had little doubt. He was one of the most driven people she'd ever met. He wouldn't stop until he accomplished his goal. Which, if she was reading it right, was to start a war. She didn't have a choice but to take his research and go to the authorities.

Taking a deep breath, she scooped up the folder with trembling hands and headed for the door. Acting like nothing was amiss, even though her heart rate was sky high and she struggled to keep from looking like she just ran a marathon, she strode from his office and back down the hall to her own. Once inside, she went into flight mode and quickly jammed things into her briefcase and threw on her coat. Slinging the case and her purse over her shoulder, she walked out of her office.

"I need to go," she told her assistant, Genevieve. "My neighbor just called and said someone broke into my house."

Genevieve's eyes widened. "Oh my goodness! Okay. Let me know if there's anything I can do to help."

Clary nodded and thanked her, continuing out the door without pause. Her heels clacked on the pavement as she hurried toward her car. Pulling her keys from her pocket, she fumbled with the fob before she finally got her shaking hand to cooperate. Unlocking the door, she threw her bags onto the passenger seat and climbed inside, pushing the button to start the car before she even shut the door.

Stark terror that Brandon would come running out the door any moment to chase her down, and what he would do if he caught her, caused her to fumble with her seatbelt, costing her precious seconds. It finally clicked into place and she slammed the car into drive. She pulled out of her parking spot, thankful she backed in that morning.

Driving out of the lot, she spared a glance in her rearview mirror, relaxing a bit when she didn't see him, or anyone else, run out of the building. She didn't know how long she had before he figured out what she had done, but she was going to make the most of it.

Clary sped through the city streets and back to her house in record time. She turned into her driveway and screeched to a halt. Grabbing her things, she scurried up the front walk and up the three steps to her porch, thrusting the key into the lock.

Inside, she dumped her bags and coat on the floor and ran upstairs to her bedroom. It wasn't safe for her to stay at her house. She needed to be somewhere neutral, where Brandon would never think to look for her.

Walking straight into her closet, she pulled her suitcase from the corner and laid it on her bed. She grabbed an armful of jeans and leggings, dumping them all in the open case, then made another trip for sweaters and t-shirts. A handful of undergarments and socks followed, along with several pajama sets and her running shoes. A quick pass through her bathroom netted her a makeup bag full of toiletries. She threw the pouch on top of the clothes and zipped the suitcase shut.

Tugging her phone charger from the wall, she pulled up the handle on the suitcase and ran back downstairs.

Not even bothering to put her coat back on, she gathered it up along with her briefcase and purse and headed back outside to her car. It only took her seconds to stow her bags in the back. Nearly manic, she jumped into the driver's seat.

Stop.

Clary took a deep breath as her subconscious yelled at her to slow down. She needed to calm herself or she was going to do something stupid. Like lead Brandon straight to her.

Pulling her cell phone from her purse, she powered it down. Her eyes roved over her closed garage door, not really seeing it, as she put her brain to work, plotting out where she was going to go.

A motel. Someplace quiet where he wouldn't ever think to look for her. And she needed to make sure she wasn't followed.

Inhaling deeply once more, she put her seatbelt on and backed out of her driveway. As she drove, her eyes darted to her mirrors every few seconds, but no one seemed to be following her. Just to be safe, she made a few nonsensical turns on her way north and west out of the city. Once she was satisfied she didn't have a tail, she ran through an ATM and took out as much cash as it would let her before she hopped on I-26 and headed inland. She didn't want to go far. Only far enough to hide until she figured out what she was going to do and what exactly Brandon had done. She needed time to thoroughly read through his research notes and figure out who to approach with the information.

Miles passed by in a blur until civilization thinned out. Her eyes caught on a sign for a small, privately owned motel. That would be perfect.

Taking the next exit, she followed the directions down the state highway until she reached the motel. She pulled into a parking spot next to the motel office and got out, making her way inside.

A young woman dressed in a light blue polo and khaki slacks smiled at her. "Hello. Welcome to Wildwood Inn. How can I help you?"

Clary forced a smile for the young woman behind the counter.

"I'd like a room, please."

"Sure. How many nights?"

"Just one for now. I'm not sure how long I'll be in town." Depending on what she found when she read a little deeper into Brandon's research, she might end up in protective custody once she went to the authorities.

Shaking off that bleak thought, she paid cash for the room and took the keycard the girl handed her. "Thank you."

The woman smiled. "You're welcome. Enjoy your stay. If you have any questions or concerns, the office is open 24/7."

Clary gave a quick nod and headed back out to her car. Her room was on the end, so she drove down to the back of the parking lot and parked in front of her door. Quickly grabbing her things, she made her way inside and shut the door.

She leaned against the solid wood for a moment, trying to calm her racing heart. Closing her eyes, she took a deep breath to steady her nerves. She was safe here. Unless he drove past the motel and saw her car, he wouldn't find her.

Feeling slightly better, Clary set her suitcase down in the chair before opening her briefcase and pulling out the file she took from Brandon's desk. Settling onto the bed, she flipped it open and started to read.

CHAPTER 3

The trill of Colin Jacob's phone pulled him from a deep slumber. Fumbling on the nightstand, he blinked the sleep from his eyes and squinted at the screen. It was his partner.

Sliding his thumb across the screen, he put the phone to his ear.

"Yeah, Ty. We catch a case?"

Ty barked out a short laugh. "I wish. I need you to come to my house. Now."

The sleep fog immediately cleared his brain at Ty's tone, and he sat up. "What's going on?"

"Hades showed up again."

"What? Why?"

"Just get here. I'll explain it all then."

Alarmed, he shoved back the covers. "I'm on my way."

The phone clicked, and he tossed it down on the bed. Dressing quickly, he strapped on his sidearm and clipped his badge to his belt. Even though they were dealing with the supernatural, somehow, the tools of his job always came in handy. He grabbed his phone off the bed and hurried to his car.

Backing out of his driveway, Colin couldn't help but wonder what the hell was going on. The last time Hades showed up, Leo lost his soul. He prayed something similar wasn't happening again, especially to Leo. The man had the powers of a god now. It could prove to be quite a fight if Hades tried something.

Hopping on the interstate, Colin pressed the accelerator, going faster than he should. His mind whirled as he drove, trying to make sense of why Hades would be back. Hecate was imprisoned in the underworld. She couldn't harm anyone anymore.

Unless she escaped.

Colin sucked in a harsh breath at the thought. He hoped that wasn't the case. The goddess wreaked havoc the last time. His friends nearly lost their lives, thanks to her. His partner's father *did* lose his life. But he didn't know what else would explain the god's reappearance.

Exiting the interstate, he followed the route to Ty and Penny's by rote, his thoughts still a jumble. Pulling through the front gate of their estate, he came to a stop in the circular drive in front of the white plantation-style house and ran up the walkway.

"Ty? Penny?" His voice echoed in the giant foyer.

"In the living room," Ty called back.

Striding quickly down the hall to his right, he turned into the first doorway and stopped short at the sight of Hades and Persephone perched on one of the sofas. Even if he hadn't been aware of who they really were, he could tell there was something otherworldly about them. There was an air about them that just felt—off.

They were also imposing as hell. Even seated, Hades was huge. He made his wife—who was not a small woman—look tiny in comparison. Colin was very glad the god was on their side. He just hoped it stayed that way.

"Okay, I'm here. What's going on?"

"A shit storm, that's what," Leo remarked.

"I figured that since he's here." Colin pointed at Hades, who rolled his eyes.

"We have a problem," Ty said. "Hecate had a backup plan. She convinced a couple minor gods—Ares's sons, Phobos and Deimos, the gods of fear and dread—to terrorize mankind. They've hooked up with a psychiatrist whose primary focus is hypnotism, Brandon Henley. The guy has his own divine ancestry. Together, they're working on a plan to cause a global war. Dr. Henley's research partner, Dr. Clary Moncrief, discovered his plan and is on the run. Apparently, it's up to us to find her and stop Henley and the gods before they can implement the plan."

Colin stared at them all in shock. "Is that all? Well, that should be a piece of cake. Hades, why are they handling all this again and not you? And where do I fit into this? Do you need me to track down Dr. Moncrief?"

"It's on you all because the Oracle said so. And you, Detective Jacobs, are likely part of the prophecy," Hades intoned.

Colin's eyes widened. "What? What does that mean? How? I'm not like them."

"Are you sure?" Hades stood and walked closer, studying Colin like he was a bug under a microscope.

Colin stared back, muscles tense. What was he talking about? The look in Hades's eyes said he knew something—something about Colin that would forever change his life. He tried to deny what he saw, but as Hades continued to stare at him with eyes that were like looking into the abyss, his palms started to sweat.

"Hades, start talking," Leo demanded, breaking the tense silence. "None of us much feel like being part of your dog and pony show tonight."

Hades grated his teeth and looked heavenward, mumbling under his breath. He looked over his shoulder at Leo. "I can still kill you, you know."

Leo grinned, completely unafraid. "Let's try it and see."

Colin snapped his fingers in Hades's face, having little patience for drama. "Hey. Forget him. What are you talking about? I have no supernatural abilities," he said, denying the feeling churning in his gut. "I've been around these four since they discovered what they are. Nothing in me has surfaced."

Hades shrugged. "Maybe the timing just wasn't right. Their abilities came to them when they were needed. Yours haven't been until now." His eyes narrowed. "I feel something in you, Colin Jacobs. I noticed it the moment you walked in."

Colin swallowed hard around the sudden lump in his throat. His gut churned harder. "Feel what, exactly?" He could not be serious.

Hades gave him a considering look. "That's a good question. Persephone, fetch that candle on the mantle, would you, my dear?"

She did as he asked and passed it to him. Hades took it and held it in front of Colin.

"Light it."

Colin's frown deepened. "Excuse me?"

"Light it."

"With what? I don't smoke, so I don't have a lighter or matches on me."

"If I'm right, you don't need them. Light it."

Exasperated, Colin reached out and touched the wick. Nothing happened.

"Your radar's off. I am *not* divine. Whatever my role is in this situation, it isn't that."

It couldn't be that. Right?

Unease skittered down his spine as something in his brain pushed against his denial.

Hades rolled his eyes again. "Please. I think I can recognize my own kind. And you weren't even trying." He held the candle out again. "Light it."

Annoyed now, Colin shrugged, shoving away the tiny voice in his head that said Hades might be right. He wasn't. But he'd play the game. Hades wanted him to try, he'd try, and then tell him "I told you so" when nothing happened.

But will you really fail? That voice reappeared, louder this time.

Shrugging off his thoughts, Colin focused on the candle, imagining it lit. Reaching out, he touched the wick.

Fire shot to life as the candle lit in Hades's hand.

Colin stumbled back. "Holy shit."

"Ha! I knew it," Hades crowed.

Ty moved closer to look at the flame. "Keira, you're not doing this, are you? It's not some hiccup caused by your pregnancy?"

Jesus, please say yes. Colin looked at her, pleading, but she shook her head, dashing his hopes of ever having a normal life again.

"The baby's sound asleep, and I would never play such a cruel trick. At least, not on anyone but Leo." She grinned up at her husband, who gave her a mock glare, one side of his mouth slashing upward in amusement.

"No, Keira did not do this, detective. It was all you. I feel Hephaestus's blood running through your veins."

Colin's mind sifted through the smattering of Greek mythology he knew. Hephaestus was the god of blacksmithing and fire. His eyes widened as he thought about what was in his garage. As a hobby to help him deal with the stress of his job, he made knives. Beautiful, flawless knives.

Persephone moved forward, staring at him and her husband in shock. "Hades, are you sure? Descendants of Hephaestus are extremely rare. Most of his line was killed off in wars millennia ago."

"He lit the damn flame, didn't he?" Hades shook the burning candle. "And you can't tell me you don't feel it too."

She pursed her lips and tipped her head in acknowledgement.

Leo came forward and surveyed Colin from head to toe before turning his intelligent gaze on Hades. "How did I not know this? I can feel everyone else's abilities. Why couldn't I feel Colin's until now?"

Hades arched one perfect eyebrow. "Maybe because you've only been a god for six months?"

Leo's eyes hardened and his body tensed.

Keira ran forward and stood between the two before they could come to blows. "Behave. Both of you. You two trying to kill each other will not help us solve our problem."

Hades looked down at the tiny hand on his chest with disdain. "Remove your hand, witch."

Leo growled.

Keira pushed him back again, then glared at Hades. "Seriously? Shove it where the sun don't shine, Hades."

"Hey!" Colin hollered again, shaking off the shock to break up the argument. "Can we get back on track, please?" It was like watching siblings fight, only if they ever actually came to blows, the scuffle would level the house.

When no one said anything, he continued.

"Let's forget about me for the moment. Where are we on finding this woman? Dr. Henley's colleague? Hades says she's in danger. Do we know where she is yet?"

With a final, pointed look at both gods, Keira walked back toward the sofa to pick up the map laid out on the coffee table. "While we were waiting for you to arrive, I attempted to locate her. I *think* she's still in the area. The stone led me to a motel just off of I-26, northwest of the city."

"She needs to be brought here immediately. It's the safest place for her," Persephone said, injecting herself into the conversation.

"How do we get her to trust us?" Penny asked. "If we go knock on her door and tell her this crazy ass story, she'll run for the hills."

"I'll go," Colin said, resigning himself to being part of this insanity. "Ty and Leo will just scare the life out of her. Keira can't for obvious reasons, and Penny's not trained for dangerous situations."

"Yeah, but she still doesn't know you or anything about you. She might think you're on Dr. Henley's side and trying to trick her. And you're not exactly the picture of butterflies and rainbows yourself," Penny argued, motioning to his muscular, six-foot-three frame.

"Yes, but I'm not six-foot-eight like Ty, and I don't give off a 'mess with me and suffer my wrath' vibe, like Leo. I'm our best chance, and I'm the only other one with the experience necessary to defend us if Henley or his god buddies find her."

Ty and Leo shared a look, then nodded.

"You need to go now, though. We don't know what Henley knows or if she was followed," Ty said.

"Okay, but before I do, someone needs to give me a crash course in this supernatural ability shit. I can feel it now, humming through my body. It's weird and I don't totally understand it."

"I know how you feel," Keira said. "That's how I felt when we figured out I was more than just a mere human. Close your eyes and look within. You'll know it when you find it. It'll tell you what you can do."

"Sounds simple enough." Taking a deep breath, he closed his eyes. Like he was searching a grid, he began looking in all the dark corners of his mind. Back and forth, up and down. Finally, a light shone brightly, beckoning him. Adrenaline zinged through his veins as he moved to take a closer look. The light grew brighter, somehow knowing it had been seen. Like a crack in a dam, information flooded his brain. Everything he wanted to know about his ancestors and how to use his abilities was there in an instant.

His eyes popped open, and he grinned.

Keira grinned back. "Did you find it?"

"Oh, yeah. And Hades, you aren't as all-powerful as you think."

Hades straightened, his shoulders going back. He arched that eyebrow again, imperiously. "I do not know what you are talking about."

Colin's smile was nothing short of wicked. "I'm not just descended from one Greek god, but from two. Somewhere down the line, one of my ancestors had children with a descendant of the god of darkness, Erebus."

Hades's eyes widened. He laid a hand on Colin's arm for a moment before drawing back.

"I feel it now. It is deep-seated within you. And very powerful. Your abilities from Hephaestus are much more freely accessible. You will have to concentrate much more to use your gifts from Erebus."

"Duly noted."

"Go. Find the woman. Persephone and I will wait here."

As he walked out of the room to go find Dr. Moncrief, Colin couldn't help but laugh at Leo grumbling about gods who thought they were entitled.

CHAPTER 4

Ripped from a deep and blessedly dream-free sleep, Clary sat up, startled; it took her a moment to register the pounding on her motel room door. Glancing at the bedside clock, her eyes widened. Who the hell was at her door at four-thirty in the morning?

Heart racing, she laid back down and slid a little deeper under the covers. Her hands trembled with fear. No one knew where she was. There shouldn't be anybody knocking on her door, let alone before the sun came up.

Her eyes landed on her briefcase, sitting atop her luggage on the lone chair in the room. She started to read through Brandon's file earlier before falling asleep. What it contained frightened her beyond measure. It shouldn't be possible, but he had simply hypnotized their patients like normal, but instead of suggesting they clear their minds and throw away the clutter so they could sleep, he prompted them to do terrible things to the animals he brought into the lab. No one could be persuaded to do something against their moral character, and they couldn't all be moral deviants in hiding. It was statistically impossible.

The pounding sounded again, making her jump. She swallowed a whimper.

"Dr. Moncrief, please open the door. This is Detective Jacobs with the sheriff's department."

She fought the hysterical laugh that wanted to break free. He was dreaming if he thought she would fall for that line. She was going to stay right here in this bed and pretend she wasn't here. Not for one second did she think he was actually a cop. She hadn't called the police yet, and Brandon certainly wouldn't have called them to report his work stolen.

Unless someone from the police was in on it, too.

That horrifying thought hit her like a punch to the stomach.

Dear God, she may not even be able to go to the authorities for help!

Tears welled in her eyes and ran down her face, soaking the pillowcase. She was so far in over her head and had no idea what to do.

"Please, Dr. Moncrief. I'm here to protect you from Dr. Henley."

Huddling deeper, she struggled to control her breathing. She didn't know how Brandon found her so quickly, but he had.

She laid there, trying to listen over the sound of the air sawing in and out of her lungs. Maybe she should get on the floor in case he decided to just start shooting.

Geez, Clary. She couldn't help but roll her eyes at herself. She watched too many crime shows. Besides, if he wanted to do that, would he really have announced himself first?

The door snicked open, then closed with a quiet click. Clary completely froze, not even breathing. How did he get in?

"Dr. Moncrief, I know you're in the bed. Please come out. I swear I'm not here to hurt you. I want to help."

Knowing she was caught, she slowly pushed the covers back. She wanted to look into her killer's face, so if she came back as a ghost, she could haunt him for the rest of his life.

To her surprise, he stood just inside the door with his hands raised, a dark silhouette against the wall.

"I'm going to turn the lights on."

She saw one arm move through the darkness to flip the light switch. She squinted against the sudden brightness and took stock of the man who had invaded her room.

Tall and broad shouldered, he was ruggedly handsome. Stubble dusted his square jaw and laugh lines fanned out from his aqua-colored eyes. His shock of light brown hair, sprinkled with gray, was disheveled, like he had run his hands through it several times.

Her eyes traveled down his torso. The long-sleeve t-shirt he wore was snug over a firm chest and around his thick arms. She bet there were some rock-hard washboard abs under that shirt too.

Continuing down, her eyes caught on the gun in the holster at his waist. A gold badge was clipped to his belt. Past all that, tight denim clung to legs that looked like tree trunks. He shifted his weight and she could see the muscles flex.

She swallowed around the lump of desire that suddenly flared to life. Another hysterical laugh bubbled up in her throat, but she firmly squashed it. Here she was, staring down the man Brandon sent to kill her and rather than wanting to bash his head in and fight for her life, she wanted to jump his bones. *What was wrong with her?*

"I know you're scared and you think I'm here to kill you, but I swear that's not the case. I need you to get your things so I can take you someplace safe."

Her eyes snapped back to his. "How did you know where to find me? How did you even know I was in danger? I haven't told anyone anything yet."

He bit the corner of his mouth briefly and looked askance before turning those gorgeous eyes back on her. "You wouldn't believe me if I told you. Not without proof. You just need to trust me for now."

She pushed the covers back further and sat up, staring at him in disbelief. "Trust you? I don't even know you. *And* you just broke into my motel room."

He ran a hand through his hair. "I don't know what else to tell you except there is much more at play here than just Dr. Henley's experiments. You need to come with me, so that one, we can protect you, and two, we can stop your colleague from unleashing his plan."

She frowned. "We?"

He nodded. "There's a group of us working to stop Henley."

"How did you know what he's doing? No electronic files on his plan exist unless he has them hidden on a personal laptop. I checked. Then, I stole the only paper copies. At least, the ones Brandon had, anyway. I don't know what he's given to anyone else."

He took a couple steps closer. "You have all of his research?" he asked, completely ignoring her question.

She nodded. "The most recent stuff, yes."

He cursed and ran a hand over the stubble on his jaw, the rasp loud in the quiet room. "He's going to come after you hard. And so are the people he's working for. We need to go. Now." In two long strides, he reached her suitcase. Unzipping it, he rummaged through it.

"Hey!" Clary scrambled off the bed. "What are you doing? Stay out of my stuff."

He thrust a sweater and a pair of jeans at her. "Get dressed."

Automatically, her arms closed around the clothes. "Wait a minute. I never agreed to go with you."

"Doc, you don't have a choice if you want to survive. The only choice you get right now is whether you want to come with me fully dressed or still wearing—that." He motioned up and down her form with one finger. His eyes took on a bit of heat as they raked over her body, clothed only in her skimpy silk sleep shorts and tank top. She knew her nipples were like little pebbles showing through the fabric, but she was powerless to do anything about it. Between the chill from the cool, late-December air he had let in and her reaction to his very masculine presence, her body was on high alert.

Arching an eyebrow at him, she opened her mouth to tell him to stuff it, but the sound of an engine roaring into the parking lot had her snapping it closed. She whirled toward the front of the room.

He motioned her to stay put and slowly crept toward the window. With one finger, he turned off the lights, then nudged the curtain aside to look out. His other hand rested on the butt of his weapon. He cursed softly and stepped back.

"Get dressed. We're leaving."

"What?" Her eyes flew to the window, wide as a dinner plate. "Who's out there?" She narrowed her eyes at him as he flew around the room, gathering up her discarded clothes to stuff them back into her suitcase. "Did you set this up to make me trust you?" She folded her arms over her breasts. "I'm not going anywhere with you."

He straightened abruptly from his task and shot her an annoyed look. "Doc, if I wanted you dead, you would be. I'm guessing all that information you took from Henley is right there in that briefcase. I could have taken it ten times over by now and left you for the flies to feast on, but I haven't, because *I'm on your side*. Now, put your clothes on so we can leave. I have no desire to get shot tonight."

Taken aback at the ferocity of his words, it took a moment for what he said to sink in. Realizing everything he said was true, she looked back at the window in horror. While she had been in here arguing with this man, the real bad guys were gathering outside. They wouldn't leave their guns in their holsters, either.

That last thought galvanized her into action. She didn't even bother to take off her pajamas. She just thrust her legs into the jeans and pulled them up over her shorts. The sweater went right over the tiny tank.

He handed her a pair of socks and her running shoes, then looped the strap of her briefcase across his chest and hefted her suitcase.

As soon as her shoes were on, she huddled behind him and peered around his shoulder as he looked out the window again.

"How are we going to get out of here?" There were two large SUVs parked catawampus in the parking lot, blocking the exit. Both were now empty, their occupants hidden somewhere out there, just waiting for her to come out.

His jaw tensed, and his mouth flattened. He glanced down at her.

"I need you to promise me that no matter what you see me do out there, you won't freeze. If we're going to get out of here, you have to keep moving."

Under no delusion that it wouldn't be bloody to fight their way out, she nodded. She just hoped the team that came to get her didn't know the detective was here. The element of surprise might be their only way through this to safety.

The sound of glass breaking in the bathroom reached them.

"Time to go," he whispered. "Stay behind me."

"No problem."

Hand on the doorknob, he hesitated. His eyes closed, and he muttered something. It sounded like, "I hope this works." Then, a zen-like calm came over him, and he let out a long breath, yanking open the door.

The first thing Clary noted was that it was pitch black outside. Not like there was no moon and a bunch of cloud cover, kind of dark, but a darkness so absolute *nothing* was visible. She couldn't see anything past the door. It felt like she was staring into a black hole.

"What's going on? Why is it so dark?" she whispered.

"Trust me," he whispered back. Unholstering his weapon, he stepped out into the abyss.

Clary tucked her hand into his waistband and followed behind. He walked confidently into the parking lot. How he could tell where he was going, she didn't know. She couldn't even see her hand holding on to him.

They only went about thirty feet before he stopped. She felt more than saw him lean in to whisper in her ear.

"We're at my car. I'm going to help you inside."

She nodded, her heart lodged in her throat. She heard the soft snick of the door opening, but still couldn't see anything. A shot rang out, and a bullet pinged off the side of the car.

The darkness blinked. That was the only way to describe it. It was like a long blink. For a split second, she could see and then the darkness was back, obscuring everything.

The detective's hand on her back propelled her forward. She found her way into the seat and fumbled for the seatbelt as he quickly threw her suitcase into the backseat and ran around to the driver's side to climb in. Another shot pinged off the vehicle and she ducked low.

She heard the jingle of his keys and the car start, but was alarmed when no lights came on inside the car.

"Why can't I see?" she asked, a bit of a frantic note in her voice. Had she been shot and didn't know it?

"I'll bring the light back in a minute. I want to get us away from here first," he said, his voice strained. The vehicle lurched as he threw it into reverse, then lurched again when he put it into drive. Gravel crunched under the tires as he sped through the parking lot. More shots sounded in the darkness, missing them this time.

"Bring the light back? That doesn't make any sense."

"I told you there was more at play than what you know."

The car bumped over uneven ground. Clary threw a hand out to hang onto the dash as he went around the vehicles blocking the drive.

"Yeah, but how do you take away light? And how the hell are you able to see and I can't?"

"It's complicated."

The car jostled some more and then evened out as he found the road. He gunned the engine and sped away from the motel.

The tires hummed as he drove at speeds far faster than she was comfortable with. Especially since she still couldn't see.

He made a hard turn. As he accelerated, Clary could suddenly see again. The car's headlights shone brightly on the road in front of them. Dash lights lit up the vehicle's interior, throwing his features into shadow. Beads of sweat at his temples glistened in the low light.

"What the hell was that?"

He took the on-ramp for I-26 east, pushing the car's engine to the max.

"You won't believe me." He swiped at the sweat trickling down his face.

"Try me," she demanded, her brows drawn down as she glared at him. "And why are you sweating? It's forty-five degrees outside." A sudden thought occurred to her. "You haven't been shot, have you?" She quickly scanned what she could see of him in the darkness for blood.

"No. I'm fine."

"Then explain what's going on."

He sighed hard. "How much Greek mythology do you know?"

Clary did a double-take. "What? What does ancient Greece have to do with any of this?"

"Everything, actually."

"Huh?" She was so confused.

"The men Dr. Henley is working for? They're not human. They're gods bent on taking over both our world and the immortal one at the behest of another god."

She knew she was staring at him like he had grown another head, but she couldn't help it.

"That's ridiculous." Clary's heart rate sped up again. She had climbed into a car with a crazy person.

"No, it's not. And it's up to us—myself and a few of my friends—who are descendants of the gods, to stop them."

"Descendants of the—seriously? You're out of your mind."

"How else do you explain my ability to impose total darkness? Or this?" He held up a fist. When he opened his hand, a ball of fire hovered over his palm.

Clary reared back in her seat, crashing into the door. Her mind whirled as she stared at the flame. She rubbed at her eyes. Maybe this was just a side effect of being in such total darkness. Her eyes were playing tricks on her.

He closed his hand, and the flame disappeared.

"I know this is impossible to believe, but it's all true. Your buddy is working for the gods of fear and dread, Phobos and Deimos. Hecate, the goddess of witchcraft, convinced them it would be a good idea to declare war on humankind. This same goddess tried to dethrone Hades six months ago. We're now dealing with her backup plan. With Dr. Henley's help, Phobos and Deimos want to send the world into chaos and start a global war. How that translates to harming the gods,

I'm not quite sure yet. Hades wasn't too forthcoming with the details. He just said to find you and bring you to safety."

Clary felt like her eyeballs were going to pop out of her head.

"The god of the underworld told you to find me? And why would Brandon and those other gods you mentioned want to do that?" she asked once she found her voice.

He shrugged. "Because they feel like it, I guess," he said, ignoring her question about Hades. "I only got a quick rundown of what was happening before I came to get you. The others might know more. I'm very new to all of—this." He swirled a finger in the air.

"How new?"

"An hour."

"You've only known about this stuff for an hour?"

He nodded. "Well, the fire and darkness part. I've known the gods were real for six months."

"Six months? But you've only been able to do—that stuff for an hour? How can you already control it so well?"

He shrugged. "The fire is easy. It's like breathing. The darkness takes some concentration, which is why I was sweating."

"How are you functional so soon after learning news like that?" She waved her hand, stopping herself. "Never mind. This is insane. None of what you said is possible. You're just a really, really good magician. And actor."

He laid a hand on her thigh. "Dr. Moncrief—Clary—this is all very real. When we get to where we're going, you'll see I'm not the only one who can make weird stuff happen."

She rolled her lips in, pressing them together. She wasn't sure what to make of any of this.

"Where are we going, anyway?"

"My partner's house. It's warded against all the weird stuff."

"Of course it is." She watched as his jaw flexed. It bothered him that she didn't believe him. She couldn't help herself, though. What he was saying—it just couldn't be possible.

Could it?

She had to admit, whatever was going on seemed to defy logic, but Greek gods? Come. On. She might have blonde hair, but did she really look that naïve?

What else explained what happened back there, though?

She crossed her arms and stared pensively out the window, unable to wrap her mind around something so, so—*illogical*. She was a scientist. A doctor. Magic didn't exist.

But what made it so dark? And how the hell did he make a flame appear in his hand?

Unable to answer either question, she just sat there and stared at the dark scenery as he drove. The miles flew by as they headed south and east toward Charleston. They stayed on the interstate through the city and were soon past its limits and headed for the Sea Islands. The bright lights faded, and the houses thinned out until they were driving through nothing but fields and marshes.

"How much further do we have to go?" she asked, breaking the silence.

"We're nearly there."

Almost as soon as the words were out of his mouth, he slowed and turned down a road that bisected two fields.

Clary sat up a little straighter, curious about where they were going. A stone wall appeared on her right that was easily ten feet tall.

"What's that for?" she asked, pointing out the window at the wall.

"It's a perimeter wall for Ty and Penny's property."

"Ty's your partner?"

Detective Jacobs nodded.

"What's your first name?" she asked, suddenly realizing she knew next to nothing about this man except he could apparently do some really weird shit. "Since it seems I'm stuck with you for the time being, I think I should probably know that detail."

A corner of his mouth lifted. "Colin. Would you like my birthdate and social security number as well?"

She glared at him through the dim interior of the car. "Very funny." She was glad he was amused by this situation, because she was not. Her mind was still trying to make sense of his tricks along with the betrayal of a man she trusted.

The car slowed again, and he turned into a drive. An enormous iron gate loomed in front of them.

"Whoa." She leaned forward to stare up at it. "How does a police detective afford a place like this?"

Colin rolled the window down and typed in a code on the keypad set into the stone. "It actually belongs to his wife. She inherited it and a multimillion-dollar ocean salvage company from her uncle."

The gate rolled slowly to one side, and he pulled through. Clary continued to lean forward as he drove them down the tree-lined driveway. Spanish moss hung from nearly every branch, giving the woods an eerie feel. Coupled with everything that happened tonight, it was hard not to imagine that the dangling strands of moss were ghosts hovering, or the fingers of death come to take her to Jesus.

Again, Clary. Too many crime dramas.

They broke through the trees, and the house that came into view was breathtaking. It was plantation-style and reminded her of something from *Gone with the Wind*. Made of brick, it had been painted white at some point. Black shutters framed the windows, and a veranda wrapped both floors. The lights in the downstairs windows were lit up, as was the ground floor porch. Whoever was there was waiting for them.

Colin brought the car to a stop in front of the house and shut off the engine.

"You ready to find out I'm telling you the truth?"

Her hand clutched the door handle. She was terrified of that very thing, because it meant everything she knew—everything she had ever believed—would be upended.

Instead of answering him, she got out of the car and walked up the steps to the front door.

Colin was right beside her. He put a hand on the doorknob and turned to look at her.

"Keep an open mind. I know it's crazy, but it's real."

She nodded once, still reeling too much from the night's events to do anything else.

He opened the door and ushered her in.

Clary stared around her in wonder. The interior of the house was as impressive as the outside. Hardwood floors gleamed in the light from a gigantic chandelier hanging in the entryway. In front of her, a staircase straight out of a movie curved up both sides of the foyer. To each side, a long hallway stretched toward the back of the house.

Colin placed a hand on her back and led her down the hall to the right and into a large living room with high ceilings.

But it wasn't the décor in this room that had her mouth agape. It was the two giant men standing on opposite sides of the fireplace, staring in her direction.

She fought to keep her face expressionless as she took in the two men, as well as the other four people in the room. The shortest of the men was blonde and seated on the sofa next to a petite woman with curly, dark hair. While his posture said he was relaxed, the look in his eyes said differently. He looked like a cat ready to pounce. Judging by the muscles she could see outlined by his t-shirt, he had the teeth to match. The woman whose hand he held looked at her curiously, with none of the danger vibes being given off by the man next to her.

The other woman on the couch had dark hair pulled back into a ponytail. Her jade green eyes were friendly, and she smiled warmly when she noticed Clary's gaze on her.

A glance across the room to the second sofa revealed another dark-haired woman who looked a bit like the first, only her eyes were dark and fathomless. She also looked extremely sad. Her entire demeanor said she was grieving, and Clary couldn't help but feel her heart tug a little at how dejected the woman appeared.

Looking back up at the men by the fireplace, the first thing she noticed was how much they resembled each other. The shorter one—and he wasn't short—had on gray athletic shorts and a plain, black t-shirt, his muscles bulging as he stood there, arms crossed. A shock of black hair fell over his forehead and into his bright blue eyes.

The other man, who looked slightly older and had to be seven feet tall, scared the daylights out of her. Wavy, black hair framed his handsome face. A black sweater fit snugly over his torso, outlining well-defined muscles. Black jeans clung to his thick thighs, and shit-kickers covered his enormous feet, adding to his height. But it was the dark look in his black eyes that had her insides quivering. This man was danger personified.

Colin's hand on her back startled her out of her perusal.

"Everyone, this is Clary Moncrief. Clary, the man in the shorts by the fireplace is my partner, Ty Farris. The dark-haired woman, there, is his wife, Penny." He pointed to the woman with the ponytail. "Next to her are our friends Leo and Keira Devereaux."

He stopped, not introducing the other two people. She turned to frown up at him.

"Who are they?" she asked, pointing at the large man next to Ty and the sad woman.

His mouth flattened and his eyes grew hard. "We'll get to them. First, you need to hear what Ty and the others have to say."

Ty stepped forward and motioned to the chair to her left. "Please, have a seat, Dr. Moncrief."

Uneasily, she perched on the edge of the chair he indicated, and speared him with a look.

"Please tell me what's going on. Detective Jacobs—"

"Colin," the man in question interrupted.

She glanced back at him, eyes squinting. "*Colin* told me in the car something about Greek gods and how Brandon is trying to start a global war. I agree he's up to something, but the whole god thing seems pretty far-fetched, even if some freaky shit happened on our way out of the motel."

Before Ty could open his mouth, the tiny woman stood and stepped forward.

"First, let me say I understand what you're feeling right now. It's unbelievable, but I promise you it's all true. Second, before we get into the nitty-gritty, you need some proof we're not all a little off in the head, am I right?"

"I tried that, Keira," Colin cut in. "She just thinks it's all a bunch of magic tricks."

She frowned. "What did you try?"

"I made it dark so we wouldn't be seen, then made this." He held out a hand, palm up. Another ball of flame hovered brightly.

Clary stared at it. It was still as unbelievable as the first time he did it.

"Okay. We'll try something more specific. Clary, if you could imagine any article of clothing for my husband to wear, what would it be?"

The blond man rolled his eyes. "Seriously, *chère*?" He sighed. "All right, lay it on me. Just nothing too obscene, okay, Dr. Moncrief?"

Mouth open in disbelief that they were actually having this conversation, she just stared.

"Well, what do you think?" Keira asked.

Shaking her head, Clary looked around at all the others. They all watched her, waiting for her to answer. Except for the giant by the fireplace. He just looked annoyed.

Deciding to play along, she looked back at Keira. "How about neon yellow jeans and a tie-dye muscle shirt?" Clary loved the eighties. *The Breakfast Club* was one of her favorite movies, along with *Sixteen Candles* and *The Goonies*.

Keira nodded. "Keep an eye on Leo."

Doing as she asked, Clary stared at the man. This ought to be good. She couldn't wait to see him stay in his jeans and t-shirt. She cocked her head, reading his shirt, and had to fight back a laugh. It had a picture of two stick figures, one with a broken back. Underneath, it read, "Oh, snap."

Giggling internally at the shirt, she was unprepared when it suddenly morphed into a tie-dye muscle shirt, revealing large tattoos on his arms. His dark denim jeans vanished to be replaced by the tightest and brightest pair of yellow jeans she had ever seen.

"Oh my God," she breathed. Rising from her chair, she scurried back several steps. *What the hell?*

"Since you're already shocked, name an animal," Penny said.

Clary looked at her, dumbfounded. "Huh?"

"Just pick one."

"Um, an aardvark."

Penny's mouth twitched. "That's a new one, but okay." She stood.

Clary shrieked when Penny morphed into an aardvark.

Frantically, she looked at Colin, who stood there stoically behind her chair, his eyes telegraphing an apology.

When she looked back at the others, Penny was standing next to Ty and Leo's clothes were back to normal.

She blinked twice. "How is this possible?"

"Because, as Colin told you, the Greek gods are real and these people are their mortal descendants," intoned the giant, whose name she didn't know.

Her eyes darted to him. His voice rolled like thunder through the room. Authority crackled through it and demanded her attention.

He walked forward until he was standing only a few feet in front of her.

She craned her neck to see his face. "Who—who are you?" she asked, softly.

Eyes serious, he stared down at her. "I am Hades."

Clary fumbled for the chair, sinking into it heavily. She shook her head in disbelief. "No. No, this isn't real. The Greek gods aren't real." But in her heart, she knew it was true. This man—god—had an aura around him that said he wasn't of this world. That he was something other than a mere man.

The sad woman came over to kneel in front of her. She laid her hands over Clary's. "Clary, I know this is a lot to take in, but we are sincere in what we tell you. I am Persephone, Hades's wife. These other people are descended from some of the most powerful gods and demigods in existence. Ty is Hades's great nephew, a descendant of Hercules. His wife Penny is also Hades's great niece, a descendant of Thetis, the daughter of Poseidon. Colin is a descendant of Hephaestus, as well as the god of darkness, Erebus. Keira is a descendant of

Hecate, the goddess of witchcraft. Her husband Leo, well, he's his own breed of god, thanks to Athena and Artemis. And you," she squeezed Clary's hands lightly, "I feel the blood of Morpheus running through your veins."

Shock reverberated down Clary's spine. She didn't know who that was, but from Hades's intake of breath, she figured he or she was important. She pushed Persephone away and stood.

"No. Nope. This is insane. You all are crazy. There is nothing supernatural about me."

Scared witless, she turned on her heel and ran out of the room. She had no idea where she was going to go. Away from here. She'd walk to the main road and get a ride back to her car. Then she'd find another motel and hide out again. Maybe drive north and find an FBI office in another state. They would want to know what Brandon was up to.

She nodded to herself as she fled down the hall and past the gorgeous staircase. That's what she would do. Go find an FBI agent away from here where just maybe she could trust him or her.

She made it to the front door before Colin's hand around her bicep stopped her.

Tears streamed down her face as she tried to pull away. "Please let me go." Her voice came out soft and broken.

He wrapped her up and hugged her to his chest. "I'm so sorry, Clary. I know what a shock this is."

She couldn't help herself and leaned into him, her emotions overwhelming her. She buried her face in his shirt and cried.

He just held her while she let out all the fear, stress, and sadness that had been her constant companions since she discovered Brandon's files.

The big hands stroking her hair and down her back helped to soothe her frayed nerves, and she was able to pull herself together after a few long moments.

With a sniff, she lifted her head. "I'm sorry. This all feels like a terrible dream. I just want to wake up."

"I know. If it helps, though, we know how you feel. I still remember when Penny showed me what she could do. I literally fell out of my chair when she shifted into a dog right in front of me." He shook his head. "It was crazy. But seeing Penny shift—that's not something that can be faked." He cradled her head in his hands, his beautiful aqua eyes staring down into hers. "Come back in and hear the rest. We can stop Dr. Henley, but it's going to take all of us."

She tried to smile, but was afraid it came out as a watery grimace. "Okay."

Sliding his hands down her arms, he twined the fingers of one hand through hers. "Come on."

Swiping at her tears, she followed him back into the room.

Clary took a deep breath and faced Hades. "Okay. Colin says y'all have a plan, but before we get into that," she looked at Hades, "why don't *you* stop Brandon? Aren't you some kind of uber-god?"

Leo barked out a laugh.

Hades shot him a look before turning back to her. "I am one of the 'Big Three,' yes." He made air quotes with his hands. "But there are a lot of factors involved as to why I can't stop your colleague on my own. For one, Persephone and I cannot stay in the mortal realm long. She shouldn't be here at all right now, and I need to get back to oversee my kingdom. We also have a—a family matter to which we must attend." His voice broke.

He cleared his throat and continued. "Last summer, the goddess Hecate tried to take over the immortal realm. Penny, Ty, Keira, and

Leo stopped her. What we did not know at the time was she put a plan in place to ensure that disruptions would continue even after she was wasting away in my dungeon. She enlisted Ares's sons, Phobos and Deimos, to send the world into chaos, knowing it would draw some of my kind who can't resist a good war into the fight. They also, acting on Hecate's direction, put my daughter, Melinoe, into some death-like state we can't get her out of and separated her soul from her body. Trust me when I say that if I could stay here and take them down, I would. I will have to be content to throw them into the depths of Tartarus with Hecate, however, once you all catch them." A strange glow emanated from his eyes. Clary felt the air in the room grow heavy. The hairs on the back of her neck stood on end. She watched the god warily, sensing he was on edge.

He paused to collect himself. The glow subsided, and he continued. "Finally, Hecate placed a spell on the twins to hide them. Keira is the only one with the knowledge to locate and possibly undo that spell."

Clary's eyes darted to the smaller woman, who listened to their exchange.

"So, what's the plan, then?" she asked him. "For Keira to find him, and then for the rest of us to round him up?"

Hades shrugged. "Basically, yes, but the details are up to you all to decide. Your fellow humans did a bang-up job of capturing Hecate. I won't stifle their creativity by devising a strategy for you. Leo would likely just ignore everything I said, anyway."

"Damn skippy," Leo said. "If I have to clean up your mess again, I'm doing it my way."

Hades growled, low and menacing. "I swear, when you finally die, I am going to make your eternal life a living hell."

Leo crossed his arms, a smug smile on his handsome face. "Good luck with that. We all know it won't be up to you where I go. You're just the keeper."

Hades lunged.

Faster than Clary had seen *anything* move, Leo sidestepped Hades's advance. It was like he blinked from one place to another.

Suddenly, cages appeared around both men.

Leo rattled the bars. "Keira. *Chère*, let me out."

Clary watched, amused, as the woman glared at her husband.

"Hell, no. You're both acting like babies. Act like the gods you are and stop poking at each other."

Leo laughed without mirth. "Have you read the stories about the things he and his brothers bicker over?"

Keira glared at him and the smile slipped from his lips. He held up his hands in supplication.

"Sorry. You're right. No matter how I feel about the bastard, we have other issues to worry about."

"Good," Keira said. Leo's cage disappeared.

"Hey!" Hades rattled his own bars. "Why does he get to be set free and I'm still in here?"

Keira cocked an eyebrow at him. "Will you behave if I let you out?"

"Yes. He will," Persephone answered, her eyes telegraphing he'd better or there would be hell to pay.

His shoulders slumped, and he nodded.

His bars disappeared. For a moment, he looked like he wanted to go after Leo again, but wisely changed his mind.

Clary waved her arms. "So, what *is* the plan? I just want all of this to end."

"Like I said—" Hades began.

She cut him off. "I wasn't asking you."

Hades sighed and looked heavenward. "Gods, help me. Are you sure you aren't related to that one?" He pointed at Leo.

Ignoring him, she faced the others.

"The first part will be easy," Keira said. "Hopefully. My abilities have been a little off, thanks to this one." She ran a hand over the slight swell of her belly and Clary noticed for the first time she was pregnant. "But the plan is for me to get past Hecate's spell and track the twins. We also need to locate your colleague. Once that's done, the rest will be up to Leo, Ty, and Colin to set a trap for him. After that, Phobos and Deimos—and possibly Dr. Henley—will be at Hades's mercy."

Clary glanced at the god, who sported an evil grin. A shudder ran down her spine. She was glad she wasn't on his bad side. She had a new admiration for Leo and his willingness to challenge Hades. If he directed that evil smile at her, she would pee her pants.

Ty grinned, his eyes on his partner. "You know, I can't say I'm sorry you're like the rest of us, Col. Now, you get to join us on our crazy adventures instead of just sitting on the sidelines watching. I know it drove you nuts over the summer to not be where the action was."

Colin scoffed. "Yeah, well, I'm not sure that outweighs being tied to him for all eternity," he said, pointing at Hades.

Hades threw up his hands. "I'm not that bad!"

"You stole my soul," Leo argued.

Clary's eyes widened. He *what*?

Hades shrugged. "I didn't feel like waiting for you all to learn about your newfound abilities. It was the fastest way to get results."

Was he serious? She understood better now why the others, particularly Leo, seemed to dislike the god so much. She would, too, if he stole her soul.

"And perhaps, if you had waited, we wouldn't be where we are right now," Colin shot back. "*Maybe* they would have uncovered Hecate's bonus plan while they took their time."

"Possibly, but it doesn't matter now." He looked at Leo. "You got your soul back. Why are we still harping on this?"

Persephone slugged him in the shoulder. "Because you're a jackass, that's why. Stop antagonizing him. I will not help you if he decides to wring your neck."

Hades huffed, and Clary smothered a smile with her hand. She quite liked Persephone.

"I feel like I've walked into a family feud," she muttered to herself behind her fingers.

Leo laughed. "You have."

She stared at the man incredulously. "You heard me?" He was clear across the room.

"God, remember?"

"Right. What are you the god of, exactly?"

He shrugged. "Myself, I guess. I'm not like them." He gestured to Persephone and Hades. "I'm mortal. Athena and Artemis gave me these abilities at birth to fulfill a prophecy, but suppressed them until I needed them. Athena unleashed them over the summer. Much to Hades's dismay." He grinned at the frowning god. "But I have all the basic powers of a god. Speed, strength, sight, hearing, along with a couple of other gifts. The biggest difference is that I can be killed as easily as any normal man."

"Thank the gods," Hades muttered. Persephone punched him again.

"Would you stop, woman?" Hades rubbed his arm.

"Stop being an asshole, and I will."

"How about we just go home? It will remove temptation." He eyed Leo like he wanted to land his fist in his face.

"That sounds like a fantastic idea." Leo clapped his hands together and motioned them toward the door. "Go do your swirly thing so you can terrorize some other unfortunate souls."

Hades's nostrils flared, and he turned. Persephone put her hands on her husband's chest and started pushing him toward the door.

"One day, you and I are going to have this out, Leo Devereaux." He walked backward only because Persephone refused to let him move forward.

Leo grinned. "Look forward to it." He waved. "Bye, now."

Hades growled.

Persephone pushed harder. "Get your ass outside, or so help me, I will call my mother."

Hades frowned down at his wife. "You wouldn't."

"Try me. I'm so tired of this. I just want to go home and find my baby."

His eyes softened, and Clary felt tears well in her own. They might be powerful deities who could do as they pleased, but right now, they were just parents looking for their lost child.

"You're right, my dear. I am sorry."

Persephone sniffed and dropped her hands. She looked around as the rest of them watched the drama play out.

"Thank you. I'm sorry he's such a jackass, but thank you for helping, anyway. Keira, when you have found Phobos, Deimos, and Dr. Henley, and a plan is in place, call my mother in England. She's running our company while I'm in the underworld. She will get a message to us so we can come retrieve them."

Keira nodded. "For what it's worth, I'm sorry about Melinoe." She placed a protective hand over her stomach. "I hope you find her soul."

Persephone nodded again, her eyes shimmering with unshed tears. "Thank you. We will see you soon." She elbowed Hades, who nodded to them all, and ushered him out the door.

The door closed with a bang as the gods left.

Clary looked around at the others, who all seemed to relax slightly now that Hades and Persephone were gone.

"They're, uh, interesting," she said into the silence.

"That's a good way to put it," Leo said.

"Did he really steal your soul?"

Leo nodded. "And gave us ninety days to find Hecate—who was in the underworld—and stop her."

Clary's eyes widened. "You'll have to tell me that story sometime. Along with the plan on how we're going to find and stop Brandon and this sorcerer." A huge yawn cracked her jaw. She was exhausted. "But right now, I'd really like to go back to bed."

Keira yawned as well and leaned into her husband. "That sounds like a fantastic idea."

Penny smiled and moved nearer to Clary. "You'll have to settle for a pull-out sofa, but it's clean. Follow me." She headed for the hall, but stopped in the doorway to look back at Colin. "Are you staying, Col?"

Clary's eyes darted to the handsome detective. Oh, how she hoped he was. Even after the crazy stuff she had watched him do, she still felt safer in his presence.

He nodded. "Might as well, since we'll probably be up in a few hours, planning how we're going to handle this situation. Thank God, it's the holidays and it was our turn to get them off. I don't know how we'd explain to the captain that Ty and I both need to take some personal time."

"You'll have to sleep down here." Penny pointed to the sofa, then looked at her husband. "I told you we should have put beds in the guest rooms."

He held up his hands. "No one ever visits us except them," he pointed to Leo and Keira.

"The sofa is fine, Penny. Just toss a pillow and blanket at me."

"I'll grab them," Ty said, moving through the group.

Keira yawned again. "Glad that's settled. Let's all go get some more shut eye. I'll start fresh, looking for our baddies once I've had a few more hours of sleep."

"Sounds good. Come on, Clary." Penny waved her forward.

With one last look at Colin, Clary followed Penny into the hall.

CHAPTER 5

The cool breeze bit into Clary's face while she sat on the bench in the dormant garden out back of Ty and Penny's house. She had come out here to distract herself. While Keira looked for the gods and Brandon, Clary once again poured over the research she took, looking for anything she might have missed that would tell her how she could stop Brandon's plan. She hadn't figured that out, but she had uncovered that there were more players in the equation. Brandon's research only dealt with the hypnosis and suggestion. It referenced a third party who would establish a large-scale delivery method. She needed to get into her lab and see if he had any other information hidden there somewhere. It would also be a good idea to talk to some of her patients. While she doubted he would be so stupid as to keep names and large-scale plans in the lab, especially after she stole the file from his desk, it would still be a good idea to look.

Sighing, she closed the folder and set it on the bench under her thigh so it wouldn't blow away. She also needed to take a closer look at herself. See what gifts her divine ancestor passed down. She'd looked up Morpheus earlier. Nothing about him surprised her. And when she thought about what she'd been able to do all her life—lucid dream—it made a lot of sense.

Clary closed her eyes and let her mind wander, hoping something would come to her. She floated, much like she did in her dreams sometimes, until a bright light shone in the darkness. It beckoned her, and she moved toward it, stopping before she reached it. Did she really want to open that door? All this still freaked her out. She wasn't sure she was ready to uncover more.

The crunch of shoes on the pebbled path took the decision away from her. She opened her eyes and looked over her shoulder to see Colin walking her way. Hands stuffed into the pockets of his coat, he stopped in front of her. The wind ruffled his hair and turned his cheeks red.

"Care if I join you?"

She slid over on the bench. "Sure."

He settled next to her and they sat there in silence for several minutes, watching the winter birds fly overhead. The sun shone brightly, but it was still chilly. A cold front came through yesterday. The rain had ended, but the cooler temperatures remained. She huddled deeper into her jacket. Now that Christmas was over, she was eager for the warmer weather to arrive. Her favorite place was the beach in the summer.

"You doing okay?" he finally asked.

Clary turned her head to look at him. "All things considered, yes. The shock has worn off. Now I'm just resigned to it all. You're taking this really well, though. Even last night, you acted like it was no big deal."

"Oh, it's a big deal, but I've also been around all this since the end of May. I didn't have the shock of finding out the Greek gods are real on top of learning I'm descended from them." He scratched at his temple and cast a side glance at her. "That last part isn't all that surprising to me, though, now that I've had a chance to process it."

Clary frowned. "What do you mean?"

"You know what Hephaestus is the god of, right?"

She nodded.

"I have a blacksmithing forge in my garage. I make knives as a hobby. I've also always had a fascination with fire. I was the EOD tech for my Delta Force unit."

Clary knew she looked like a fish, gaping at him. But she wasn't sure what surprised her more—the fact he knew how to defuse bombs, or the fact he had been Delta Force.

The latter, she decided, looking back out over the trees. Most definitely the latter. He just seemed so mild-mannered. So unlike what she imagined such an elite soldier to be. Leo, she could see in that role. His whole being shouted badass. Ty, too. But Colin was just so—controlled.

Although she could see how that control would serve him well as a bomb disposal tech.

His laughter had her turning again.

"What?"

His smile was bright. "You look so shocked."

"Frankly, I am. You just don't seem the type."

Colin shrugged. "I never intended to be Delta. It just kind of happened."

She arched a brow. "How do you just 'happen' into Delta Force?"

He gripped the back of his neck and sighed. "I liked bombs. Had a good aptitude for them. My CO told me if I didn't put in for Special Forces, he was going to make my life a living hell. I believed him. And it intrigued me. I spent three years in Special Forces before I got a selection notice for Delta. I could have turned it down, but again, I liked bombs."

"How long were you in?"

"Delta?"

She nodded.

"Ten years."

"That's a long time. What made you leave?"

"My dad got sick. Pancreatic cancer. My mom was having a hard time taking care of him alone." He shrugged. "They needed me more than the military. I was at the end of my enlistment term, and had twenty years in, so I came home."

"And now you're a detective. How old are you?"

"Forty-one. I was thirty-eight when I left the military."

"And your dad? Did he make it?"

Colin shook his head. "He died about six months after I came home."

She laid a hand on his arm. "I'm sorry. I know how rough that is. My dad died about ten years ago. Plane crash." At thirty-three, it still hurt to think about him. "He was on a business trip. I'm just thankful my mom wasn't with him. After I moved out, she accompanied him most of the time and would go sightseeing in whatever city he was in. But she stayed home that trip because she wasn't feeling well."

"That's rough. At least I got to say goodbye to my dad."

Clary nodded and sniffed back the tears. "Yeah. It was worse for my mom. She felt so guilty about staying home. He was coming back early for her."

Shoving thoughts of her dad away, she changed the subject. "So why a cop? Why not something like demolition?"

"I liked the defusing aspect of bombs, not so much the setting of them."

"Do you still defuse bombs?"

"Sometimes. When I started with the department, that was my specialty. But I found I really liked the investigative part of police work, so I took the detective exam and aced it. I still teach bomb disposal and act as a backup for the other EOD guys, though."

Clary studied Colin in a new light. It seemed the detective was much more than just an investigator. Those aqua eyes held a keen intelligence and a fearlessness she hadn't seen until now. She was glad he was the one who came for her last night. He made her feel safe, just being near him.

"How are things going inside? Is Keira having any more luck?"

A smile tipped one side of his mouth. "Not really. Seems the baby's acting up today more than usual. Must feel his momma's stress."

"The baby's a boy?"

Colin shrugged. "They don't know yet, but they keep referring to it as a he, so maybe they can sense it. Or they don't want to refer to the baby as it, so they picked a pronoun. I think Keira mentioned she has an ultrasound scheduled soon after they get back to Louisiana, so they should know for sure soon."

Clary frowned. "They don't live here?"

He shook his head. "No. Keira and Penny are both originally from Texas. Leo is from Louisiana and owns a camping and survivalist outfitter there."

"How did they all meet, then?"

"Ty and Leo served together on the same SEAL team. Penny met Ty when her uncle was murdered and she inherited this property and his business."

"Murdered?"

"By Hecate—well, her minions anyway—for Hippolyta's belt, of which he was the guardian. His death made Penny its keeper. Ty and I were investigating her uncle's death, which is when Ty found out who he is."

"How do Keira and Leo fit into that? Hades said it was the four of them who defeated Hecate."

"At the time of Theo's death—Penny's uncle—they didn't know who was after the belt, so the investigation took them to Greece and then to Texas where Penny's from. They picked up Keira there when Penny's house was attacked. The three of them fled, but needed a place to lay low. Leo's house is in the back of beyond, which made it perfect."

"And you? What was your role in all that? I mean, it was a murder investigation, right?"

"I mostly ran interference with our captain to keep him off Ty's back. And no one but Ty and me really believed Theo was murdered. Most indicators, besides a few anomalies on his autopsy findings, were that he died from an accidental fall. Other than that, I did some digging for information when they needed it."

"And now, you're in the thick of something otherworldly again, only this time as one of them."

He nodded once. "So are you. Welcome to the club."

She smiled ruefully. "It's one I'd rather not be a part of, thanks."

He patted her hand. "It won't be all bad. You'll come away from this with some great friends."

Clary looked down at where his big hand still rested over her smaller one. Her heart skipped a beat at the sight. In the light of day and not running on adrenaline, her attraction to him was just as potent, which didn't really surprise her. She'd always been a sucker for the intelligent ones. The fact he was also handsome as the devil, and apparently, a badass ex-Delta Force soldier, only added to his allure.

"I know you're scared, Clary."

She glanced up at his words. He was still looking out over the yard, his face in profile. "But I promise to do everything I can to keep you safe." He turned his head and their eyes met. That silly little flutter started up in her chest again. His sea-colored eyes were intense in their sincerity.

She held his gaze. "I know." And she did. It was crazy, but she trusted this man implicitly. She didn't know how, but she knew he would always do what was in her best interest.

When he lifted his arm and motioned her closer, she didn't hesitate to scoot over and tuck herself up against his side. The feel of his arm, heavy across her shoulders, was welcome and left her feeling protected. She leaned her head into his shoulder and laid a hand on his chest, staring out at the dormant garden as she soaked up the comfort he offered.

CHAPTER 6

Clary's hair tickled Colin's lips as it fluttered softly against his face in the December breeze. She felt good in his arms. He hadn't intended to invite her so close, but looking at her sitting there, her golden hair shining in the sunshine, his hands had itched to run his fingers through it. He just wanted to be close to her. She was a calm moment in an otherwise chaotic world.

He had been ready to tear his hair out inside. Until Keira could get a handle on her abilities, they were spinning their wheels a bit. Finally, Ty suggested they try to track Brandon down the old-fashioned way. Talking to Clary about where the man might be was the first step to that, and Colin volunteered to go find her and ask. Not only did he want to get the information, but he also wanted to check in on her and make sure she was doing all right. She looked a little shell-shocked last night.

He also just wanted to see her. To be near her. It had been hard to let her out of his sight when they all retreated to bed for another few hours. It felt wrong. He'd never had such an intense, immediate desire to protect a woman in his life.

His world felt right now, though, holding her. Which was insane, because outside of this moment, the world wasn't even close to being right.

That thought brought him back to why he sought her out in the first place. Closing his eyes briefly, he inhaled the fresh, citrusy scent of her hair. He didn't want to interrupt their moment, but the longer he waited, the longer Brandon Henley eluded them.

He pulled back slightly so he could look down at her. "Clary. Do you have any idea where Dr. Henley might go?"

She sat up and his arm dropped from around her shoulders. "Not really, no. He was a bit of a loner. And he doesn't have any family. His parents are dead and he's an only child."

"No girlfriend?"

"Not that I know of. He dates, but it's never anything serious."

"Do you know where he lives?"

She nodded.

"Good. Saves me having to break the rules and run a DMV search to get it. Unless Keira comes up with something, Ty, Leo, and I are going to go over there tonight and do a little recon."

She held up a finger. "One problem with that. I don't know the actual address. I just know how to get there. And I've only been there once. We had to pick up a colleague from the airport. Brandon forgot some files at home, so we swung by to get them."

Colin leaned forward, elbows braced on his knees, and pinched the bridge of his nose. That put a bit of a wrench in their plans.

He turned to look at her. "Can you tell me how to get there?"

She shook her head. "I can tell you the neighborhood, but not what street or how many houses down it was. It's off I-26, north of the airport. It wasn't all that long ago, so if I go there, I could find it again."

Colin weighed the risk of taking her with them versus the risk of leaving her here and doing a DMV search instead. Those searches were tracked, and with no active case against Henley, it could come back to bite him on the ass. Not only could he lose his job, but it could bring attention to this case. While a rogue scientist planning to start a war was usually something he would share with his department and the feds, in this case, the fewer who knew, the better.

He stood abruptly.

"Come on." He held out a hand to her.

She frowned up at him, but put her hand in his, grabbing the folder beneath her leg with the other. He tugged her to her feet.

"What are we doing?"

"Going for a drive." He started for the house, not releasing her hand. It felt too good nestled in his own. "You'll probably remember how to get there better during the day than tonight in the dark. Besides, I don't really want you along for what we have to do later. It's safer if you stay here."

He towed her inside, eager to finally have something to do besides wait.

With a quick explanation to the others about what they were up to, Colin led Clary outside to his jeep.

The drive into the city was a quiet one. His mind was too busy running plans and scenarios for what they might find at Henley's house for him to make conversation. Neither of them broke the silence until they were on the interstate, heading northeast.

"Colin, something's been bothering me since you found me at the motel. I know how *you* found me—Keira—but how did Brandon and the gods' lackeys find me? I wasn't followed. I made certain of that."

That had been bothering him as well. "Was your phone on?"

She shook her head.

"Did you take the battery out? It's possible to turn it on remotely if the battery is still in it."

Her eyes widened. "No. I didn't even think about doing that." She crossed her arms and huffed. "I should have thought of that. What good does it do me to watch all those crime dramas if I'm just going to act like an airhead?" she grumbled under her breath.

Colin laughed. "Give yourself some credit. You were under a lot of stress when you checked into that motel. You did the right thing by not staying home."

Suddenly, her eyes widened. "Shit." She scrambled for her purse. "I still have it on me."

He kept one eye on her and one eye on the road while she rummaged through the bag.

"God, I'm so stupid. I led them straight to us." She paused her search, looking up at him, eyes wide. "What if they're at Ty and Penny's now? Planning a way to get inside?"

Colin laid a hand on her arm. "Clary, relax. There is no safer place than their house. Leo has that place wired from top to bottom. An ant can't crawl across the driveway without him knowing about it. And if you're worried about Phobos and Deimos doing something—other-worldly—Keira took care of that. If you aren't supposed to be there, you aren't getting in undetected. Unless you're Hades or Zeus or some other equally powerful god."

She bit the corner of her lip and nodded, then resumed her search. Finally, getting frustrated, she upended the entire thing on her lap. All sorts of feminine stuff poured out, covering her lap and falling to the floorboard on her side of the car.

She picked her phone up off the top and pushed the home button. It lit up, showing her home screen.

Curses that he rarely heard from anyone except his old military friends flew from her mouth. She mashed the power button to turn it off, then ripped off the back and pulled out the battery, throwing the whole lot into her lap with a disgusted huff.

Colin fought the grin that wanted to break free. She was cute when she was angry.

"Feel better?"

She glared at him, huffing once more before her shoulders relaxed and a self-deprecating smile crossed her lips.

"I know I'm overreacting a bit, but I'm a lot smarter than that."

He took her hand, running his thumb over the soft skin soothingly. "Stress makes us all do stupid stuff. It's how we handle it that matters."

"Well, apparently, I rip apart cell phones and curse like a sailor."

He grinned at her. "You'd fit right in with my old unit."

She laughed and shook her head. "My mom tried to curb my tongue. I can't help it, though. Some things just require stronger words."

Her expression turned somber, and she turned her hand in his, clutching it tight. "But seriously, are we going to be okay since my phone was on?"

He threaded his fingers through hers, liking the feeling of her hand in his. "We should be fine. They don't know where we're going. They might be able to guess, but they don't know for sure. They also don't know if you're alone or with someone else."

Her hand flexed in his.

He squeezed back. "Relax. We'll be okay. After last night, I think any attempts they take to get to you will be planned and not something spontaneous. They know you've got some serious backup now."

She inhaled, then blew out the breath slowly. "Okay. I'll try to curb the freak outs."

"You can still freak out, but just remember you're not alone."

She squeezed his hand. "I know."

They rode in silence for several miles before she directed him to take an exit into a neighborhood north of the airport.

Unerringly, she guided him through the housing development to a small, ranch-style house. Colin glanced at it as he drove past. It was a far cry from what a twisted individual like Brandon Henley should live in. This was a nice neighborhood, where children weren't afraid to ride their bikes or run around outside with their friends. It made him sick to think that Henley lived in their midst.

He circled the block before parking on the street several houses down from Henley's. It didn't appear like anyone was home, but the door on the single-car garage was closed, so it could be hiding a vehicle.

"Stay here." He opened his door. "I'm going to see if anyone's home."

"Be careful."

He nodded once and climbed out of the jeep, sliding a pair of sunglasses on his face. Surveying the neighborhood around him from behind the dark lenses, he casually strolled down the sidewalk toward Henley's house. He walked straight up to the front door and knocked, fully expecting there to be no response.

After several moments of waiting, he walked along the front of the house and around to the side of the garage. There was a window set high on the wall.

Backing up a few steps, he ran forward, using his momentum to boost himself up. He grasped the windowsill and peered inside. It was empty, just like he thought it would be.

Dropping to the ground, he wandered around the back of the house. A quick glance revealed a sliding door as the only entrance. He knocked on it as well, so anyone watching would think he was just trying to contact Dr. Henley and not casing the place. While he waited for a response to his knock, he looked inside. The door opened into the dining and kitchen area of the house. There were papers scattered on the table.

Colin wished it was dark so he could get in to look at them now.

Walking around the other side of the house, nothing else stuck out to him. He strolled through the grass and headed back to his car.

"Anything?" Clary asked when he climbed back inside.

He shook his head and started the engine. "Not really. He's got a bunch of papers strewn all over his table, but there are no signs of life. If he's still in town, he's staying somewhere else."

"So, now what?"

He pulled away from the curb. "Now, we wait until it gets dark and hope he doesn't come back for all those papers in the meantime."

CHAPTER 7

For the second time that day, Colin found himself parked on Brandon Henley's street. This time, though, he didn't intend to stay outside.

Exiting his car, he, Ty, and Leo made their way down the sidewalk. Stepping into the shadows cast by the large oak in Henley's front yard, Colin called on the darkness to shroud them as they gained entry into the house.

"That's frickin' cool," Leo said. "It looks a bit like the bubble Keira uses to shield us." His gaze wandered around them, seeing something Colin and Ty could not.

"Let's get moving," Colin said, sweat popping out on his brow. "This thing takes some concentration to hold. Hades was right. My abilities from Erebus, while powerful, are buried deep."

Quickly, they moved across the yard and around the side of the house to the sliding glass door. Colin pulled out his lock picking kit and made fast work of the lock. The three men entered the house, closing the door and window blinds behind them.

A quick scan of the room revealed a burglar alarm next to the door.

Ty cursed, moving toward it, only to realize it wasn't armed.

"Dude left in a hurry," Leo commented.

Colin nodded, dropping the cloak he had put over them. He shook out the tension from his shoulders and walked over to the table that was still scattered with papers. He clicked on his flashlight and began rummaging through them.

"Anything good?" Ty asked.

Colin frowned, staring down at the documents. "Maybe. These look like plans for a bomb."

Ty and Leo both came over to see what he found.

Leo picked up a sheet and started reading. "This isn't just any bomb." He pointed to the page. "They got their hands on nuclear material."

"Jesus," Ty said. "Can you imagine what would happen if they set off several of these all over the world?"

Colin's gut churned just thinking about that. They needed to end this before it got out of control.

"Let's fan out," Colin said, putting the paper he held on the table. "See if we can find a clue about where Henley may have fled. Or who else he's working with. It can't just be Phobos and Deimos. They're soldiers, but not strategists like their father. There has to be a human running the show."

Leo and Ty both headed to check out the rest of the house while Colin kept going through the documents on the table. It was all just dispersal rates based on wind patterns in different locales. Gathering them all up, he folded them in half and tucked them into a pocket on his cargo pants. Clary would want to see them. Maybe she could help them determine where they would strike first.

"Hey, guys," Ty called from the living room. "Come take a look at this."

Colin entered the living room to see Ty standing in front of a bookshelf, holding a picture frame.

He turned it so Colin and Leo could see.

"Henley has a boat."

Leo groaned. "He could be anywhere."

Colin agreed. "Take the picture. Maybe Keira can get a location on it."

"If the baby cooperates," Leo said. "He's not even born yet and is already giving us fits."

Ty lifted a brow. "What the hell did you expect? It's your kid."

Leo rolled his eyes, a happy smile quirking one corner of his mouth. "I know."

Colin grinned at the exchange. "Come on. Let's finish searching, so we can get this info back to Keira and Clary."

They fanned out and continued their search. Colin tore through Henley's bedroom, although there honestly wasn't that much to go through. The man was meticulously neat. The mess of papers on the table was an anomaly, which made him wonder why Henley left them there. Maybe to send them down a rabbit hole to keep them occupied while he enacted some other part of his plan. He just hoped Henley and his counterparts weren't actually planning a nuclear strike. Or if they were, they hadn't gotten very far in the process. He needed to contact some of his old sources and put out some feelers. See if anyone heard rumblings of someone building a dirty bomb.

Finishing the bedroom and attached bath, he headed back out to the living room.

"Find anything?" he asked.

Ty and Leo both shook their heads.

"Let's get out of here, then. We need to find that boat. The sooner we get moving on that the better."

Concentrating hard once again, Colin summoned the darkness to shroud them as they made their way back outside. Although, looking at the sky, it may not have been necessary. Storm clouds had gathered, plunging the world into shadows.

Lightning flickered ominously. Leo paused in the front yard, staring into the darkness, his eyes looking for things only he could see.

"What?" Ty asked. "What do you see?"

"Nothing. But the energy is off. Something's not right."

The hair raised on the back of Colin's neck. He felt it too. There hadn't been a cloud in the sky when they went into the house, and there wasn't any bad weather in the forecast.

"You know, I've been reading Dad's mythology texts, trying to bone up on stuff. There was a story in one of them that said Zeus gave Phobos and Deimos lightning and thunder once." Ty glanced at the sky. "I'm wondering if maybe they didn't give it back."

Colin frowned, then handed Leo the car keys, knowing he had the fastest reflexes of all of them. "You drive."

Not wasting any time, the three men ran to Colin's jeep, piling inside. Leo pulled away from the curb with a squeal of the tires. Lightning continued to flicker all around them as they hightailed it south.

They made it to the interstate before the first bolt crashed down yards away. Leo jerked, but didn't slow down. Another bolt hit the road in front of them, sending asphalt flying. He swerved to avoid the hole, but continued to rocket down the highway.

"Jesus, Leo," Ty said. "Slow down." His white-knuckled grip on the chicken bar matched Colin's as Leo dodged a slowing car.

"Do you want to end up like a fried rat? Because I don't." Two bolts came down in succession right in their path. Leo maneuvered them through with deft hands.

Colin cringed as Leo quickly switched lanes again to avoid the cars that had come to a halt. He was thankful it was the middle of the night and traffic was light. This drive would be a lot more harrowing if there was more traffic. "I'm rethinking letting you drive."

Leo's eyes flickered to the rearview mirror. "We're being followed."

Colin and Ty turned to see a set of headlights keeping up with them.

Another bolt came down only feet ahead of them. The electricity made the hair on Colin's arms stand on end. His ears rang from the boom that shook the car. He held onto the chicken bar as Leo dodged to the right around the hole.

"We need to stop them. They're getting really close with those lightning bolts," Ty said.

Colin took a deep breath and closed his eyes, visualizing a dark shroud around the other car.

"Whoa," Ty muttered. "That's something else. The car just—disappeared."

"It's still there. It's just hidden. They can't see us now, so take the next exit, Leo."

Leo sped up again, reaching the exit in record time. He raced down the off ramp, barely slowing, and merged onto the surface street at seventy miles-per-hour.

Colin felt the sweat pop out on his forehead. His heart raced faster the further away they got from the other car. He closed his eyes and tried to shut everything else out while he concentrated on keeping the vehicle in the dark.

He felt Leo make several sharp turns, moving them deeper into the residential areas and away from the interstate.

"I think we lost them, Col." Ty said. "You can probably lift the darkness now."

Colin expelled a breath and opened his eyes, feeling the weight of his ability leave his shoulders as he let it go.

"That ability of yours is going to come in handy, I think," Leo commented as he drove them south through the city.

Colin was beginning to see that and understand why Hades said this would take all of them to stop Phobos and Deimos.

"You know what I don't get?" Ty said. "Why didn't they try to take us out at Henley's? Why follow us?"

"Maybe they need Clary," Colin said.

"For what?" Ty asked.

Colin shrugged. It was just a theory.

"And don't they already know where she is?" Leo said. "You told us someone tracked her phone, and that she didn't realize it until this morning. If they wanted her, they could just come after her at the estate."

Colin shrugged. "Maybe they're trying to figure out what they're up against. We might not be as powerful—except for Leo—but there are a lot of us."

"Whatever the reason, we need to stay vigilant. They caught us unaware, and that makes me nervous," Leo said. He slammed his hand against the steering wheel. "Keira and I need to find a way to make the baby behave. The sooner she can remove the cloak Hecate put on Phobos and Deimos, the better off we'll be."

Colin agreed. But how were they supposed to make an unborn baby behave?

***

When they arrived back at the estate, the downstairs lights were all on. Leo parked the car and the three men filed into the house. They found Penny and Clary in the living room, poring over Henley's research.

"Where's Keira?" Leo asked.

"Upstairs," Penny replied. "She said the baby's sleeping, so she's attempting to locate the spell Hecate placed on the twins."

Leo nodded and ran up the stairs to find his wife.

Colin turned to Clary. "I've got some new info for you." He pulled the packet of papers from his cargo pocket and held it out to her.

"What's this?"

"Plans for a nuke. I know you aren't a weapons expert, but it might help you figure out what he's planning."

Clary unfolded the papers and immediately began reading. Her eyes widened with each page.

"This is bad. The research I took is all about convincing normally mild-mannered people to do terrible things. He could hypnotize someone to carry one of these and we'd never suspect who it was. It could literally be anyone. I need to get into my lab and see if he left anything behind. I took the research on his desk and checked his computer, but I didn't have a chance to check his office or the lab area before I ran. There might be some clues there, especially if he left in as big of a hurry as I did."

"Okay," Ty said. "Once it's light out, Colin, take Clary to her lab. Clary, don't let on to the staff that anything untoward is happening. As far as they're concerned, you're coming in to finish up some things before you take a leave of absence."

Clary nodded. "How do I explain him?" She pointed at Colin.

"Boyfriend," Colin immediately replied. "I'm traveling with you and it was quicker for us to stop on our way out of town than it was for you to go in and then come back to get me."

She blushed as she looked up at him. Biting her lip, she nodded.

"Good. That's settled. Now, I don't know about the rest of you, but I'm ready to go to bed. It's been a long-ass day," Ty said.

Colin agreed; but after all they'd been through and all that was to come, he had a feeling sleep would be elusive.

CHAPTER 8

Nerves churned through Clary's gut as she waved her badge over the pad at the entrance to her lab. The door buzzed and the lock clicked open. She grasped the handle and pulled, letting them inside. Her heart thudded in her chest. It was a risk to come back here. She didn't know if Brandon had set up an alert to let him know if she showed up at work. Two days ago, she would have said he didn't even know how to do that, but since he had somehow turned her cell phone on remotely, she wouldn't put anything past him.

She led Colin over to the security desk so he could get a visitor's badge.

"Hi, Dr. Moncrief," the guard greeted her, accepting Colin's ID. "What are you doing here on a Sunday?"

Clary offered him a tight smile. "My boyfriend finally managed to get some time off. My research is at a stage where I can leave it for a bit, so we decided to take a spur-of-the-moment trip. I just came in to check on a couple things and make sure everything is squared away for Genevieve while I'm gone before we leave." She motioned to Colin. "I brought him with me because it made more sense than coming in here, going all the way back to his place, and then coming back this way again. Besides, he wanted to see where I worked."

The guard nodded. "Well, I hope you have a good time."

"I think we will, thank you. By the way, you haven't seen Dr. Henley today, have you?"

He shook his head. "No. Were you expecting him?"

Relief and disappointment both flooded her. She wasn't ready to confront Brandon, but the sooner they found him, the quicker this would be over. "No. I tried to call him earlier to let him know I decided to go out of town, but all I got was his voicemail. I was going to talk to him while we were here if he was in the building."

"Sorry, doc. I haven't seen him. If I do, though, I'll let him know you were looking for him."

"That would be great, thank you."

The guard nodded and turned to entering Colin's information into their system. It didn't take long before he was handing Colin a visitor's badge and a pen so he could sign the log.

Clary quickly scrawled her name next to his before giving the guard a nod of thanks. She ushered Colin toward the door to the guard's left, where she scanned her badge again, letting them into the main part of the facility.

She led him down the long corridor to a door at the end. Through the large window in it, she could see that the lab was empty, exactly what she was hoping for.

Scanning her badge once again, she let them in and went straight for the bank of cabinets along the wall to her left.

"What are you doing?"

"If I wanted to hide something, I'd do it in plain sight. This is where we keep basic supplies for our patients. Many of them need fluids and IV medications while they're here." Grabbing a pair of gloves from the box on the wall, she pulled open the first door. Boxes of saline-filled syringes, IV tubing, and other basic medical supplies greeted her.

"What do you want me to do?" Colin asked.

"Look bored. There are cameras pointed at these cabinets. You aren't authorized to touch any of this stuff."

Out of the corner of her eye, she saw him lean a hip against one of the stainless-steel work tables and cross his arms over his chest.

"I'm okay to be in here, though?"

She nodded. "So long as I don't leave you alone, yes. We allow family and friends in here during patient drop off, so it's not restricted access."

"How long have you worked here?"

"Five years."

"Seriously? How old are you?"

"Thirty-three. I graduated high school at sixteen, college at nineteen. I couldn't fast track much through med school and residency, though. I finished those at twenty-five. I did a stint at Johns Hopkins where I completed my fellowship in psychiatry before I came here."

She crouched to look at the items on the lower shelves. After a moment, she noticed his silence and looked back at him. He was staring at her with an incredulous look on his face.

"What?"

He cleared his throat and straightened. "I had no idea you were some kind of genius. I guess I shouldn't be surprised. Hades said most of the gods' descendants are highly intelligent."

Clary frowned as she considered that. She had never thought much about why her brain was the way it was before. It was just her. It made sense, though, that her ancestor could be the reason she was a genius.

She shrugged and went back to looking through the vials. "Well, I'm grateful. I like my brain. It's helped me to make a difference in the world."

"We know what your partner's been working on, but what about you?"

"Me? Pretty much what Brandon's *supposed* to be doing—studying the effects of hypnosis on sleep. We take terminally ill patients who struggle with sleep because of pain or anxiety and hypnotize them to fall asleep, planting the suggestion that they'll get a full night's rest and feel refreshed when they wake up. Theoretically, it should help them, but I've been getting complaints it's not working. That, in fact, they wake up feeling worse. Now I know why."

"Did you have any success at all?"

She reached into the back of the cabinet, rummaging through the last set of boxes. "Some. I was encouraged after the first few weeks of the program. They all responded well. Even reported they had more energy. Then everything changed a few weeks ago. I thought it was just a fluke in the data. That the subjects weren't achieving full hypnosis and therefore not sleeping as well as in the beginning. It's why I was so anxious to look at this week's data set and went into Brandon's office to find it."

She closed the cabinet and moved to another one. "I still don't understand how he's doing what he is."

"What do you mean?"

"Contrary to popular belief, hypnosis won't make you do something you normally wouldn't. It relaxes barriers in the mind, but it won't remove moral boundaries. What he made these patients do did that. It shouldn't be possible."

Colin sighed and arched an eyebrow. "Yeah, well, there are a lot of things going on that shouldn't be possible."

Clary huffed and opened a box of bandages. "No kidding."

The lab door swished open and Clary whirled, fully expecting to see Brandon or those gods he was working with standing there, ready to take them out. Instead, it was a fortyish man in a charcoal suit.

"Hello Dr. Moncrief. Detective Jacobs."

Colin had straightened and turned at the intruder. Clary took several steps toward him, seeking the protection of his bulkier frame.

"Who are you?" Colin demanded.

"How did you get into my lab?" Clary asked.

"The guard let me in." He pulled a wallet from his pocket and opened it. A gold badge glinted in the overhead light. "My name is Luca Vasco. I'm with the FBI."

Her heart thudded in her chest.

"How do you know who I am?" Colin interrupted. "Or is it me you're looking for?"

Agent Vasco spared him a look and shook his head before turning his focus back to Clary.

"Dr. Moncrief, I need to speak with you about some research that has come out of this lab."

She shared a look with Colin.

"My research is all above-board," Clary said. "I'm studying the use of hypnosis on terminally ill patients. I've published my preliminary findings in several academic journals."

"Yes, but your partner's research is—shall we say—suspect?"

"He's been working on the study as well. I can assure you I've seen his research, and it is as sound as mine." It wasn't, but she wasn't about to admit that. No one outside of their circle needed to know what was happening. They'd suspend her medical license, then lock her up in an asylum for even suggesting it.

The agent walked further into the room, stopping on the other side of the worktable where Colin had just been leaning. "I'm not talking about the sleep study research, Dr. Moncrief. I'm talking about his other research. The stuff you were looking for evidence of in that cabinet." He motioned to the cupboards behind her.

Clary froze. Like a deer in headlights. She didn't know what to say or do. No one should know about Brandon's research outside of their little circle.

Colin noticed her inability to talk and stepped in. "How do you know about Dr. Henley's research? And you still haven't answered my question about how you know who I am."

Agent Vasco sighed. "I know who you are because of who your friends are—namely Penelope Dimas."

Colin frowned, confused. "What? What does Penny have to do with anything? She's as clean as they come. She shouldn't be anywhere near the fed's radar."

"She's not. She's on my radar."

Colin's frown only intensified. "Okay. I think maybe you should explain, because I am thoroughly confused. If you're not here in an official capacity, then why are you here? Or are you here in an official capacity, but also keeping tabs on Penny for some other reason?"

Agent Vasco held up a hand. "It's not what you're thinking. I know that Dr. Henley has been attempting to develop a way to create an army willing to do whatever he wants. I've been keeping tabs on him, but he slipped my surveillance two days ago. I haven't been able to pick him up again."

Shocked, Clary moved around Colin. "Wait. You've been investigating Brandon? But unofficially?"

He nodded.

"Why?"

The agent pinched the bridge of his nose. "Because I know that what he's doing isn't just about the war he wants to create."

"How?"

"Because I'm one of you."

CHAPTER 9

C olin stared at the dark-haired man standing on the other side of the table. His eyes held a wary resignation, but no deceit.

"Look, I know you want answers, but I'd rather only explain this once. And Penny will understand it better than any of you."

That just confused Colin more.

"You're going to have to give me something, because I'm not about to expose all our security measures without some proof."

Agent Vasco stared at him for a moment before grabbing a beaker from the table and moving over to the sink in the corner. He filled the container about halfway and returned to the table. He looked at Colin and Clary.

"Just so we're on the same page, we're talking about divine power, right?"

Colin nodded and saw Clary do the same.

"Good." Agent Vasco tipped the beaker, pouring some of the liquid into his other hand. But instead of pooling and dripping over his palm, it formed into a ball. He set the beaker down and used both hands to manipulate the water, pulling it into a long, thin rope, swirling it, and squishing it back into a ball before sending it back to the beaker.

"Poseidon?" Colin asked, cocking a brow.

Agent Vasco nodded. "By way of Theseus, an ancient king of Athens. I'm stronger than a normal man as well."

"Christ," Colin muttered. "How many of us are there?"

"Many more than you would think, detective."

"How do you know about us? She and I just found out about our own abilities."

He looked at Clary. "As a king, Theseus held company with many of divine lineage. One of his mistresses was a daughter of Apollo, which is where my family comes in. Apollo, among many things, is the god of oracles. This is where what Penny knows comes in. It has to do with her past. Look, I need to talk to all of you. Can we take this back to her estate?"

Wary still, even knowing what the agent could do, Colin pulled out his phone. "I need to make a call first."

Agent Vasco nodded. "By all means."

Colin turned to Clary. "Keep searching through the cabinets. I'm going to verify his identity quickly."

Moving to a back corner, but keeping an eye on the agent, Colin pulled up his hacker friend Charisse's number and hit send.

It rang twice before she picked up.

"Let me guess. You need me to search for something."

Colin smiled ruefully. "You know me so well."

She laughed. "What do you need?"

"I need you to look up a name for me. Luca Vasco. Claims he's an FBI agent."

He heard her keyboard clack as she typed.

"Luca Thomas Vasco. Thirty-eight. Six-foot-two, two-twentyish. Born in Austin, Texas to Madeline and Thomas Vasco. One younger sibling. Studied law at The University of Texas before joining the FBI. He's currently with the Charleston, South Carolina field office."

"Wait. Did you say Austin?"

"Yep."

"Is there a connection between him and Penelope Dimas or Keira Artherton?"

He heard more clacking of her keyboard while she ran the search.

"No. They lived in the same city, but their families didn't live anywhere near each other."

"What about between his parents and Ajax and Phoebe Aeolia? Or Costas and Larissa Dimas."

There was another long pause.

"That's interesting."

"What?"

"His mother is—for lack of a better term—a psychic and an herbalist. I've got some business records here that show that Phoebe Aeolia spent at least some of her time while she was a teenager working for the woman."

Colin kept his face expressionless, but nonetheless, his eyes flicked to the FBI agent standing across the room, watching Clary hunt through the cupboards.

"Okay, that's what I needed. Thanks, Charisse."

"No problem. Stay out of trouble."

"No promises."

Colin ended the call and wandered back over to where Clary was closing the last of the cupboards.

"Who was that?" she asked.

"An old friend who is very, very good at getting information quickly."

"What did you find out?"

His eyes traveled to the man watching their exchange. Colin addressed him as well as Clary. "That he has a connection to Penny, so I'm inclined to believe he's on our side."

"I am," the man answered.

"Good." Colin turned to Clary. "Did you find anything?"

Her shoulders drooped, and she shook her head. "No."

"Is there anywhere else in the facility he could have stored something?"

She shrugged. "Maybe. I don't even really know what I'm looking for."

"Have you checked his office?" Agent Vasco asked.

"No. We haven't had a chance yet."

Agent Vasco spun on his heel. "I'll go check his office, since the guard thinks I'm here in an official capacity. You two tear this place apart."

He was out the door before either of them could respond.

Clary stared around the lab. There were a handful of workstations that needed to be checked. She looked up. Colin's eyes followed hers. "We should check behind the ceiling tiles, too."

"Janitorial keeps a ladder in the supply closet." She pointed to a door on the right side of the room.

He nodded. "Go get it and start searching. I'm going to go check yours."

Surprise made her pupils dilate. "You think he hid it in my office?"

"It'd be the last place you would think to look, right?"

She straightened. "Yes." She shoved a hand in her pocket, pulling out a set of keys.

He took them from her and gave a quick nod. "Start searching. I'll be back."

She was heading for the closet as he turned and walked out of the lab. He hurried down the corridor, passing Vasco in Henley's office, and reading nameplates as he went until he found Clary's. Using the keys she gave him, he quickly found the right one and unlocked her door.

He gave it a once over. Bookshelves lined one wall, full to the brim. The wall behind her desk had mounted horizontal cabinets, some of them open and spilling their contents from their depths. Her desk itself looked like a paper factory had exploded over it. Piles of paper, files, and books littered its surface. The floor around her desk wasn't much better. Stacks of books and file folders that wouldn't fit on her shelves sat in little towers around the room.

Taking two long strides, he reached the bookshelf, quickly checking to see if all the books were flush against the back of the unit before edging it slightly away from the wall to look behind it.

Finding nothing, he turned his attention to the chaos of her desk and cabinets and decided to tackle the cabinet first. Lifting open the first door, he slid it into its slot in the shelving unit and sighed at the mess. He should have expected this. When he found her at the motel, her stuff had been everywhere and she had only been there a few hours. Apparently, it was true what they said about geniuses being messy.

Trying not to screw up her "system" any more than necessary, he rummaged through the mess of file folders and binders. He found several pens and other random office supplies, but no notes or files that didn't look like they belonged.

Moving on to the desk, he sat in her chair and pulled open the top drawer. Poking through it, all he saw were more office supplies. She had a ton of blank post-it notes. He could understand why. They peppered the cabinet doors and the wall between the shelving unit and the desk. None of the scribble on them made sense to him, though. A lot of it was in a shorthand that probably only she understood.

He yanked open the second drawer. More files met him. He paged through them, skimming each one long enough to see they were just scholarly articles on sleep and dreams. He scooped the whole mess out and checked the bottom of the drawer, finding it empty.

Returning the files, he pushed the drawer closed and grasped the handle on the third and tugged, only to find it locked.

Fishing Clary's keys from his pocket, he found one that looked like it would fit and shoved it in the lock. With a quick flick of his wrist, he was in. He yanked open the drawer, fully expecting to see more files. This drawer, though, was mostly empty. There was a folded blanket and a small fan.

He removed the fan, then picked up the blanket. As he lifted it out, something tinked onto the metal bottom of the drawer. He looked down and felt his heart skip a beat.

A metal cylinder about the size of a cigar slowly rolled to a stop in one corner.

Commotion in the hallway drew his attention. It sounded like footsteps. And a lot of them.

Quickly, he grabbed the cylinder and thrust it and Clary's keys into his jeans pocket, then shoved the blanket and fan back into the drawer, closing it hurriedly. Thinking fast, he took his phone out of his pocket and dialed Ty.

Just as the line connected, the door to Clary's office opened and several cops stood there.

The surprise in their eyes rapidly turned to suspicion, and they drew their weapons.

Colin held up his free hand.

"Whoa! Hold up. What's going on?" Colin frowned at the officers.

"Sir, we need you to hang up the phone."

"Ty, I'll have to call you back," Colin said into the phone over the sound of Ty asking what the hell was going on.

He ended the call and laid the phone down on the desk.

"I'm Sergeant Hazelwood with the Charleston PD. What's your name? And why are you in Dr. Moncrief's office?"

"Colin Jacobs. I'm a detective with the sheriff's department. Clary's my girlfriend. We stopped in here so she could check on some things on our way out of town. She said I could use her office to call my partner while she did her thing down in the lab. What the hell are you guys doing here?" His mind whirled as he tried to figure out why there were suddenly cops in Clary's lab.

His thoughts went to the object hiding in his pocket. It suddenly made a lot of sense why Brandon hid it in Clary's office.

"Do you have some ID?" Hazelwood asked instead of answering Colin's question.

"It's in my back pocket." He shifted so the officers could see what he was doing and pulled his wallet out, along with his badge. He handed both over.

Hazelwood flipped open his wallet and looked over his shield before radioing dispatch with his information.

"You gonna tell me what this is about?" Colin asked again, although he had a good idea what that was.

"We got a report that Dr. Moncrief was hiding a small amount of nuclear material with the intent to construct a dirty bomb."

Colin fought to keep his expression neutral. The cylinder in his pocket suddenly felt like it weighed a hundred pounds. "Uh-huh. And was it Dr. Brandon Henley who called you?"

The sergeant's eyes widened in response. Before he could reply, the radio squawked as the dispatcher replied to the inquiry about Colin's identity.

"Badge number confirmed. Subject's record is clean."

"Well, detective. It seems you may have picked the wrong woman to date."

Colin scoffed and folded his arms over his chest. "Hardly. I think you'll find she's done nothing wrong."

"Well, we still have a search warrant for her office and lab."

"Have at it, gentlemen." He picked his phone up off his desk and walked toward them.

They parted to let him through.

"Stay here in the hallway," Hazelwood said, eyeing him suspiciously. He turned to one of his colleagues. "Simmons, go get Dr. Moncrief from the lab and bring her back here."

As the officer turned to do as he was told, Agent Vasco walked out of Brandon's office, stopping the younger man in his tracks. His immediate frown had all the uniformed officers standing straighter.

"What's going on here?" He held up his badge. "Special Agent Luca Vasco, FBI."

Hazelwood's eyes widened before he pulled his shoulders back and puffed out his chest. "We got a tip that Dr. Moncrief was in possession of enough nuclear material to make a bomb."

"From Henley," Colin said over the man's head.

Vasco's eyes flicked to Colin's briefly before he speared the officer with a death glare.

"Did you ever stop to consider that maybe that's what Henley wants you to think? I've been on that man's trail for weeks now. I don't think it's a coincidence that as soon as he slips my surveillance, he's trying to cast suspicion onto the woman who ratted him out in the first place."

Hazelwood frowned. "What?"

"You've got the hiding nuclear material part right, but the wrong doctor. Dr. Moncrief isn't the person you're looking for. Dr. Henley is."

"Why weren't we informed of your investigation?"

"Because right now, all I have is a bunch of intelligence that suggests he *might* have done something."

"We're going to need to see that intelligence."

Vasco gave a curt nod. "Of course. I can give you want isn't classified. It's back at my office, but I'll have it faxed over as soon as I get back there."

"We also need to talk to Dr. Moncrief."

"I'll get her." Colin pushed past the deputies before one of them could make their way down there. Clary needed a few details, so they didn't give these officers a reason to doubt the story they were spinning.

He strode down the hall and rapped on the window to get Clary's attention. She was on all fours, her head buried in one of the lower cupboards, butt wiggling as she rummaged through the cabinet. He couldn't help but feel a pang of disappointment when she backed out of the cupboard and turned around, hiding her nicely rounded rear from his view.

He motioned for her to let him in.

She hurried over and pushed the button to unlock the door.

He stepped inside, but didn't let the door close. When she opened her mouth to speak, he laid a finger over her mouth, not knowing if any of the Charleston PD officers were within earshot.

She frowned up at him curiously.

"The cops are here," he said, voice low. He dropped his hand. "They got a call from Brandon saying *you* were hiding nuclear material."

Her eyes widened.

"Did you find anything?"

She shook her head. "But I haven't been through everything yet."

"Okay. I think Vasco can talk them out of searching, or at least *thoroughly* searching, but they still want to talk to you."

"What do I tell them?"

"That you contacted Vasco several weeks ago because you suspected Henley was up to something. You agreed to let him in the building while you searched before you and I headed out of town for a brief getaway."

She nodded.

"Oh, and they think Vasco has the file you took from Henley's office."

"Got it."

He took her hand and led her out of the lab.

The others all turned as he and Clary approached.

"Dr. Moncrief?"

"Yes. What's going on? Colin said Brandon's trying to pin his misdeeds on me."

The officer nodded. "He called us and said you were hiding nuclear material here. In your office, to be precise."

Alarm bells went off in Colin's head. If they searched the office and failed to find anything, they might want to search him since he was the last one in there. He edged closer to Vasco.

"Well, he's wrong. You're welcome to search."

The officer looked up at Vasco. Colin could tell it was chafing for the deputies to relinquish control of the investigation, but because

Vasco was already on scene and stating that Clary called him in several weeks prior, it was Vasco's case.

"Officers, I can assure you, you're barking up the wrong tree. I will send you the file when I get back to my office, but Dr. Moncrief is right. If you'd like to search her office, I don't have a problem with that."

"We'd like to look through the lab as well."

"That's fine, so long as it's on your warrant."

Hazelwood handed Vasco a set of documents. "I think you'll find it's all in order." He looked back at Simmons. "Suit up and go check the lab. Take Mathews with you."

The man nodded and walked away, another officer in tow.

"You won't mind waiting here while we go through your office?" Hazelwood asked, turning back to Clary and Colin.

Clary shook her head.

The sergeant and his remaining officers donned disposable suits and gloves, then filed into Clary's small office. Colin took the moment of distraction to slip the cylinder he found in the drawer into the pocket of Vasco's suit.

Vasco's only reaction was a quick dip of his head and a moment of brief eye contact.

Hazelwood rattled the bottom drawer of Clary's desk.

"Dr. Moncrief, do you have a key for this drawer?"

"Yes." She looked up at Colin. "It's on the key ring I gave you."

He pulled the keys from his pocket and stepped inside to pass them to the sergeant.

Hazelwood selected the same key Colin used only minutes ago and put it in the lock, pulling the drawer open. It only took him a moment to lift the blanket and fan to see that it, too, was empty of anything incriminating.

Colin leaned against the wall and crossed his ankles, waiting for Hazelwood to come to the conclusion that Henley was blowing smoke up his ass.

Within minutes, the officers stepped back into the hallway, shutting Clary's door behind them.

Hazelwood handed Clary her keys, then looked at Colin. "Would you mind turning your pockets out, detective?"

Colin arched an eyebrow. "Seriously? Whatever happened to professional courtesy?"

Hazelwood smiled without mirth. "This is it. I could put you in cuffs and search you. We're dealing with a matter of national security. I don't take that lightly."

"Neither do I." Eyes telegraphing that he was pissed, Colin straightened and thrust his hands into his pockets, pulling them inside out. He held his hands up at chest height. "Happy?"

Hazelwood just arched a brow and looked at Clary. "Dr. Moncrief, could you do the same, please?"

With an exasperated huff, she handed Colin her keys and shoved her hands into her pockets, pulling on the lining to expose it. She crossed her arms over her chest and glared at the older man.

"I told you, you were barking up the wrong tree," Vasco said.

Hazelwood offered a tight smile. "Yes, well, we take threats like these very seriously. So seriously, that I contacted the FBI's Charleston field office, and they knew nothing about this matter."

"I asked him not to say anything yet," Clary said. "What we do here—it's sensitive work. We study dreams and hypnosis. Fields that often get a scornful look from members of academia, and downright laughter from normal citizenry. If it got out that a hypnotist was attempting to create a dirty bomb, it wouldn't matter that it was separate from his work. It could ruin the credibility of any study the lab conducted for years to come. I would have to scrap everything and start over. Luca's an old friend of Colin's partner's wife, Penny. I asked him to look into it discretely and if he thought it warranted more resources, then we could make the investigation official." She held her hands out in supplication. "I just didn't want to throw away years of research if it turned out to be nothing."

Simmons and Mathews stepped out of the lab then and made their way back to the group congregating outside of Clary's door.

"Anything?" Hazelwood asked.

They shook their heads.

"There's nothing in there that could hide nuclear material. It's all boxes of medical supplies and other various office equipment. And yes, we checked in the boxes," Simmons said.

Colin could see Hazelwood's jaw work as he clenched his teeth, frustration clear on his face. "What the hell was his goal in sending us here if there's no evidence?"

"My guess is that he knows I'm onto something and he's trying to buy himself some time to get away with the nuclear material," Vasco replied.

A reluctant acceptance crossed Hazelwood's face, and he nodded. "You'll keep us informed? I don't like that this is happening in my city."

Vasco nodded. "Of course. Now that we have this incident, I think it's time I made my investigation official. I'll speak to my SAC and get back to you."

Hazelwood nodded. "I'll put out an all-points-bulletin for Dr. Henley." He turned to his officers. "All right. Come on, boys. Let's go."

CHAPTER 10

C lary held her breath until Sergeant Hazelwood and his officers were through the door that led to the lobby. As soon as it closed behind them, she let it all out in a rush and leaned her forehead against Colin's arm for a brief moment.

"He's getting desperate," she said.

Colin nodded.

"What I don't get is why he sent them here and they didn't find anything. I know him, and he wouldn't send them on a wild goose chase. He meant for them to find something."

Vasco reached into his pocket. He removed the metal cylinder and held it up. "And they would have if we hadn't searched first."

Her eyes widened. "Where did you find that?"

"I didn't. Colin did."

"Where?"

"The bottom drawer of your desk."

Her mouth worked, but she couldn't make the words come out. Closing her eyes, she ran her hands over her face.

"How did he get it in there? It was locked. So was my office, for that matter."

Vasco smirked. "I picked the lock on his office door in about three seconds."

"And those drawer locks are pathetic. They're meant to deter an opportunistic thief. If someone really wanted in there, all it takes is a YouTube video and a thin piece of metal," Colin added.

She made a face. "So, what do we do now? This just turned into an official investigation."

"I'll do exactly what I said I would and fax the redacted file to the Charleston PD."

Clary's brow furrowed. "But it's not redacted."

He smiled. "Yet. We're going to block out most everything. Particularly the stuff about his hypnosis research. Even that, I'm going to keep out of my SAC's hands. The story you told about not knowing for sure if Henley was really up to anything was perfect. I don't have to give them much because they don't think we know much."

Colin reached for his phone. "I'll call Ty and have Leo run the file over here."

Vasco laid a hand on Colin's arm. "Have him meet us somewhere neutral. I'm not a hundred percent certain Hazelwood believed us. He probably left an officer or two outside to follow us when we leave here."

Clary ran her hands over her face again. "This is such a mess."

Colin laid a hand on her shoulder. "We'll get it straightened out. There's seven of us and only three of them."

She knew he was right, but at the moment, in the thick of it, it felt like such a huge undertaking. They had to take down two ancient gods, all while the FBI and local cops looked on now. She hoped Agent Vasco had a plan to keep everyone in the dark about what was truly happening.

CHAPTER 11

C olin thumbed open his phone, calling Ty. He picked up on the first ring.

"Colin, you're on speaker. What's going on? Is everything okay?"

"Yes and no. We ran into a bit of an issue at Clary's lab. Long story short, Henley's gotten the authorities involved and is trying to pin things on her. The good news is, we found his planted evidence before the cops. There's also a fed here—Special Agent Luca Vasco—who knows what's going on."

"Going on? Like for real, what's happening?"

"Yep."

"How is that possible?"

"He's like us, and it has something to do with Penny and a connection between their families. I don't know all the details and he insists on explaining things when everyone's present. Right now, though, I need Leo to run the file Clary took from Henley's office to that barbeque joint—Sunny's—near Magnolia Plantation. We need to give something to the authorities and we need to do it quickly. Agent Vasco told the cops he had it at his office and that he would fax it over as soon as he got back there. We're still at the lab, but we'll be heading out soon. I'll text you when we leave."

"Got it," Leo said.

"Once we get the file, Clary and Vasco are going to redact the most damning stuff, then she and I are going to head back to the estate. He can meet up with us there after he sends the pages to the local cops."

"Sounds good. We'll see you soon."

Colin ended the call and slid his phone back into his pocket.

He held out a hand to Vasco. "Give me the cylinder. I'll put it in the safe at Ty's house."

Vasco handed over the tube.

"Let's get going." Colin tucked it into his jeans, praying it was shielded and he wasn't doing irreparable damage to himself.

CHAPTER 12

C lary leaned her hands on the edge of the sink in the bathroom at Ty and Penny's. She had retreated upstairs when they returned to the estate, needing a moment to herself to collect her thoughts.

She stared at herself in the mirror. Her face was pale and her eyes worried. She hadn't stopped shaking since the cops showed up. She had a genuine fear they wouldn't find Phobos and Deimos in time to stop them. She doubted that tube of nuclear material was all they had. Brandon wouldn't leave it behind to frame her if it was. God help them all if they failed.

She turned on the taps and washed her hands before splashing some on her face, hoping it would give her some color and wash away a bit of the fear in her eyes. This was so far out of her realm of expertise. She didn't know what to do other than trust those around her. With three former Special Forces soldiers and an FBI agent, they should have some idea what to do, at least.

Patting her face dry, Clary opened the door. Colin leaned against the wall, muscled arms crossed over his broad chest. A lock of his light brown hair fell over his forehead. Her belly clenched as she took him in. He was, by far, the sexiest man she had ever met.

"Hey," he said, straightening to step toward her.

Clary craned her neck to look up at him.

"You doing okay? You looked pretty flustered."

She nodded. "I won't lie and say I'm not terrified we won't find them in time, but I'll be all right. It just makes me more determined."

He brushed back a strand of her hair that had come free of her ponytail. Her face tingled where his fingers touched and her breath caught at the intense look in his Caribbean blue eyes.

"Good." His hand slid along the side of her face to cup her head. He lightly grazed her jaw with his thumb. Clary's heart rate leaped at the soft touch.

"We're going to stop them. With all of us working together, they don't stand a chance."

She covered his hand with her own, taking a moment to enjoy the feel of his warm hand against her face.

"I know."

She swayed toward him, her pulse speeding up. She wanted him to kiss her. Wanted to know if he felt the same insane spark of attraction as she did. As crazy as it was, it was the one normal thing in her life right now. She could handle being attracted to this man. Everything else? That was still in question.

Slowly, his eyes locked on hers, he leaned closer. Clary could feel the pull, drawing her in like a magnet as he advanced.

Mere inches away now, she closed her eyes.

"Colin! Clary!"

She jerked at the sound of Ty's deep voice booming up the stairs.

Colin cursed softly and pulled back. His hand slid down to rest against her neck.

"What?" he called back.

"Vasco's here."

"We'll be right down."

Clary's eyes met his once again, and she swallowed hard. His thumb brushed against the throbbing pulse in her neck, pausing. He stared down at her, his eyes glittering. She stared back, unable to look away.

Finally, he leaned down and placed a gentle kiss on her forehead. His lips, warm and soft, lingered on her skin.

Clary closed her eyes and savored the contact.

He straightened, letting his hand fall away, and stepped back.

"Come on. Let's go see what Agent Vasco has to say."

She nodded, inhaling a deep breath through her nose to steady herself, and turned for the stairs. She was still shaky, but now for an entirely different reason.

Trying to shove her emotions into a box in her brain to deal with later, she scampered down the stairs to the living room, where the others gathered. There would be time enough later—after they stopped Brandon and his sidekick—to figure out what to do about how she felt about a certain, sexier than sin police detective.

She perched on the sofa next to Keira, while Colin sat on the arm next to her. Vasco was seated in a chair flanking them.

"We're all here now, so please explain how you're involved. How do you know me and my family?" Penny said.

"Your mother—your real mother, Phoebe—worked for mine at her shop when she was a teenager. My mother's side is where I get my abilities. We're descendants of Theseus, a son of Poseidon. We're also descendants of Apollo. We have his gift of prophecy. As clichéd as it sounds, my mom is psychic."

"Are you?" Keira interrupted.

He tipped his head. "To a degree. I get some intense 'gut feelings' that I've learned never to ignore. But Mom knows things she shouldn't. Like with your mother, Penny. She knew Phoebe's life would end tragically, leaving you behind. She made sure to put Costas

Dimas in Theo's path because she knew you would need a good home."

"Why didn't she do something if she knew my parents were going to die?"

"Because it wouldn't have mattered. Death still would have found a way."

Leo shifted on the sofa next to Keira. "This idea that our lives are controlled by some unseen fate still chafes. Makes it feel like we're all pawns in someone's game to do with as they please."

"But it's what we do in the life we're given that matters. How and when we die might be predetermined, but what we do with our lives and how we conduct ourselves isn't."

"Okay, so your mother knew about Penny's parents. How do *you* know about who we all are and what Henley's up to?" Ty asked.

Clary leaned forward slightly, wanting to know the answers to those questions as well. Brandon wouldn't have bragged about what he was up to, and she hadn't told anyone except the people in this room.

"Mom had a vision about Phobos and Deimos. That they had come to destroy mankind. She saw Henley's face as well, but didn't know who he was, so she drew him, then asked me to find out who he was. I ran her sketch through the FBI's facial recognition software and got a hit. When I realized he was here in Charleston, I knew whatever was happening would involve the four of you." He motioned to Ty, Penny, Keira, and Leo. "I already knew who you were because, one, Mom's been keeping tabs on Penny for years, and two, because of what happened with Hecate. She saw all of that and kept me in the loop. I started following Henley and kept my mom apprised of everything. She told me about Colin and Clary."

"Your mother's the one who gave me that horrible tea when I was three, isn't she?"

Vasco nodded. "It was to protect you."

"How did she know my adoptive parents?"

"Costas's grandmother and my grandmother were friends. Our parents grew up together."

"Did your mother's vision happen to say whether Phobos and Deimos succeed?" Colin asked.

Vasco shook his head. "No. Just that the threat was there. She gets feelings and visions about big events, but rarely knows their outcomes. Individuals, though, she can hone in on, especially if it's a close friend. Ironically, though, she can't see or feel anything about her own future or that of her kids and husband."

"That's probably not a bad thing," Clary said. "I don't think I'd want to know when my children were going to die."

Vasco smiled. "That's what she always says."

"So, what's our game plan, Agent Vasco? How do we stop Dr. Henley and the twins, but still keep the authorities at bay? They're going to want in on this. We're talking terrorism here," Keira said.

"It's Luca, please. And I have the police handled. Charleston PD will be easy to stonewall. This is a federal case by its very nature. As for my colleagues, my office is currently short-staffed, so I'm working without a partner at the moment. Our SAC is a bit absent, which works in our favor. So long as I feed him the standard 'I'm working on it' line and nothing bad happens, he'll be happy. He thinks I'm coordinating with local law enforcement to track down Dr. Henley."

"He won't check up on you?" Colin asked.

Vasco shook his head. "No. He's very much a politician. He wants updates, but unless something isn't running smoothly, he really couldn't care less."

Clary stared at him, appalled. How could someone in such a position care so little?

"How do you work for a guy like that?" Ty asked.

"Normally, he drives me crazy with his brown-nosing, but today, I'm thankful for it. It makes all of this much simpler."

"Will Hazelwood be content being stonewalled?" Colin asked, naming the sergeant they encountered at Clary's lab.

"He won't have much of a choice. And even if he calls my SAC, all he'll get is a promise that I'll call him with an update."

Colin scoffed and just shook his head. "Okay, so we're in the clear on that front. What's our plan to go after the bastards?"

"I've been thinking about that," Leo said. "Keira got a location on Henley's boat while y'all were out. It's docked in Charleston Harbor." He looked at Clary. "Would he stay on the boat? I mean, he has to know we'll look into anything in his name."

Clary frowned. "He's arrogant, so he might believe he's untouchable. Especially with Phobos and Deimos on his side."

"You know what I still don't understand?" Ty asked. "Why Henley agreed to this. He has to know that what they're planning, wiping out mankind, he's part of that."

"I'm betting they told him he would be spared," Clary said. "Brandon likes life. He is far from suicidal and he has no martyr ideologies. He probably thinks he's going to survive this."

Ty scoffed. "He won't. Hecate would have made sure of that. I'll be surprised if she intends to let Phobos and Deimos live if this plan succeeds."

"We can use that if we catch up to Brandon. Somehow convince him he won't live through this no matter what they told him."

Colin felt the press of time weighing on them. "We should probably head out. Check out his boat and see if he's there. The longer we wait, the longer they have to plan."

"Agreed," Leo said. "But I'm not going with you."

"What?" Ty said.

"The rest of you need to go, but Keira needs to stay here and I'm not leaving her unprotected. The stunt with Clary, they're getting bolder."

Ty groaned. "I get that, but Leo, you're the only one with the strength to take on a full-fledged god. We'll need you if the twins are there."

"You've got Colin now. And Agent Vasco—sorry. Luca. They may not have my strength, but they've each got skills of their own. Combined, I don't think you'll have a problem. And, if things get dire, you can call me. I can be anywhere in moments."

"Hold up," Luca held up a hand. "I'm sorry. I might know you all are descended from the gods, but I don't know what any of you can do besides Penny. How can you take on a god all by yourself? We all only have a fraction of their abilities."

"Because I'm not like the rest of you. Athena and Artemis gave me the powers of a full-fledged god at birth and suppressed them until they were needed. Athena unleashed them when we had to deal with Hecate. I'm still mortal, though."

"Seriously? Why don't you just run up there then and deal with them all? The rest of us can stay here and keep an eye on your wife."

"Because it's not all about strength and speed. If I was dealing with Hades or Ares, it would be a fairly even contest. Phobos and Deimos can control Zeus's thunderbolt. I can't fight them if I'm dodging lightning. And they'll likely target me because they know I'm the biggest threat. We figured that much out when we fought Hecate. She could lob giant chunks of her house at us, so we had trouble even getting close to her. It took all of us working together to win."

"He's right," Penny said. "Keira can feed us information from here and she shouldn't be left alone unless absolutely necessary. We can't rely on her being able to defend herself. Stress seems to make the baby act up more." She looked at Ty. "You know you would argue to stay behind if it was me."

He pressed his lips together and nodded. "Fine. Leo is out. The rest of us should gather what we need to cover all contingencies."

"We should take two cars," Colin said. "In case we need to split up."

Leo stood. "I'll run home and get the comm units. You might need them to coordinate."

"Bring some extra ammo, too. I've got some here, but not enough for all of us," Ty said.

Leo nodded. Before Clary could blink, he was gone. Just poof! Gone. The sound of the door was the only sign he hadn't simply vanished into thin air. She stared at the spot where he was moments before and just blinked.

Keira patted her knee. "You get used to it."

She swung her gaze to the younger woman. "I don't know why I'm so shocked. Nothing about the last two days has been normal."

Keira laughed. "It'll go back to normal—well, a new normal—soon enough."

Ty scoffed. "Yeah, until Hades shows back up and throws everything into chaos again."

"Hades?" Luca said. "Wait. He was here?"

"Oh, yeah. Showed up at three in the morning two nights ago and said he needed our help. This still stems from the debacle with Hecate. It's her backup plan. She was determined to take the bastard down. Unfortunately, that means we're part of the solution this time too. I hope this is the last time. I'd like to find our new normal and stick to it too."

Luca stared at him wide-eyed. Clary knew how he felt.

"Mom didn't mention that part."

Ty clapped his hands together. "Let's go gather what we need. It won't take Leo long to get back. Then we can come up with a plan to get on board that boat."

Luca pulled his keys from his pocket. "I need to run home and change. I have a go-bag in my car, but it's only got more of this in it." He motioned to his more formal attire.

"You're about Leo's size," Keira said. "You can borrow some of his clothes if you'd like. He won't mind."

"All right. I guess that works."

She stood. "Come on. I'll show you to our room and you can pick through his things and take what you want."

Ty and Penny followed them out of the room, leaving Clary alone with Colin.

"So, what now?" Clary asked. It seemed they had some time to kill. She didn't like being idle.

"How about we find some lunch? It might be our only chance to eat before we enter a marathon planning session."

"Food sounds good." And it did. She could go for a big bowl of mac and cheese—her go-to comfort food when she was stressed—but she'd settle for anything, really. She'd been too nervous to eat breakfast before they left for her lab.

Colin led her out of the living room and down the hall to the kitchen. He went straight to the fridge and pulled open the massive door to reveal its fully stocked shelves.

"Do you want ham, turkey, or roast beef?" He opened a drawer. "It looks like there's some pasta salad in here, too."

"Turkey's fine."

"Cheese?"

"Sure."

"What kind?"

"Whatever you're having. I'm not picky."

He took several packages from the drawer, then closed the fridge.

"Can you get the bread? It's in the pantry." He pointed to a door behind her.

Clary turned around and opened it, then looked around in wonder as she stepped inside. Floor-to-ceiling shelves lined the walls and were laden with various foodstuffs. She loved to cook. If she had a pantry like this, she would never leave her kitchen.

"Grab some chips or something too. I want something salty."

She jerked at the sound of his voice so near, and looked over her shoulder to see him standing in the doorway.

He motioned to a shelf. "Grab what you want before Ty gets down here. Your choices will diminish by at least half once that happens."

Clary laughed.

He smiled back, his eyes crinkling at the corners with mirth. "I'm serious. It takes a lot to fuel that giant body of his. He's always eating."

She believed him. Ty easily weighed two-fifty, and it was pure muscle.

Footsteps sounded in the hallway, heralding the arrival of the man in question.

"Jacobs, are you stealing all my food?"

"Yep."

Clary smiled as Ty rolled his eyes.

"Save me some jerky. And don't touch Penny's oatmeal cream pies. She'll kill you." He smiled at Clary. "You can take whatever you'd like, though, Doc."

"Hey," Colin protested.

Ty shrugged and reached around him for the trail mix. "She's a guest."

"So am I, jackass."

"You spend as much time here as you do your own house."

"Your weight room is better."

"The cooking isn't, unless you're the one doing it." He turned to Clary. "Half the crap in here is so he can cook meals at my house. I love my wife, but she can't cook for shit. Neither can I."

"See," Colin said. "You'd starve if it wasn't for me."

Clary laughed and snagged a bag of chocolate-covered berries from the shelf and some pretzels, then ducked under Ty's arm.

"Uh-oh, Col. Your girl's abandoning you."

Clary laughed. "I want to keep my lunch. He's on his own."

"Smart woman," Ty said, elbowing Colin in the ribs.

Their laughter abruptly died as an alarm blared through the house. Clary put a hand over her racing heart and glanced out the window.

"Why the hell is that going off?" Colin said.

"I don't know. Let's go check the security feeds." Ty tossed the box of trail mix on the counter as he ran past.

Unnerved, Clary ran after them, wanting to know what was happening. Penny and Keira were coming down the stairs, Luca on their heels, as they crossed the foyer to go down the other hallway.

"Keira, call Leo and find out how close he is," Ty hollered.

They hurried into a den-size room down the hall from the living room. Clary stopped just inside the doorway, amazed at the sight that greeted her. Luca skidded to a halt behind her.

"Holy shit," he muttered.

Holy shit was right. Monitors lined one wall, each screen split into four, covering different areas of the house and grounds. A desk that spanned the length of the room held a host of communications equipment that looked like something straight out of mission control.

Ty sat at the desk and pulled up a screen on the computer.

Luca stepped around her, eyes locked on the scrolling data. "What's that?"

"Sensor data. Leo has the entire estate wired." He scrolled down the list until he came across one that was flashing red.

"There." He pointed at the screen. "Something tripped the perimeter alarm on the back of the property."

Picking up a remote control, he pressed a couple buttons and the monitors on the wall changed, each one now displaying a single image of the estate. It had started to rain and lightning flashed. Clary heard thunder echo through the house, even from this interior room.

"Maybe it was the weather that tripped the alarm," she mused.

"Unlikely," Ty said. "Leo accounted for stuff like that." He pressed another button and all the feeds rewound several minutes to just before the alarm went off.

Clary watched the video play. All the screens showed various sections of the stone wall that surrounded the property. The only movement was the flash of lightning and tree leaves in the wind from the storm.

Suddenly, one camera shifted, almost like a strong wind knocked it loose, but none of the tree branches in the frame bent accordingly. Ty rewound the feed and played it again, slowly. This time, Clary saw two figures cross the top of the wall, still a blur even at such a slow speed.

"Shit! They got past the wards without a blip." Ty stood and whirled, his eyes landing on Keira. "How close is Leo?"

"He should be back any second."

"Good. You get to the safe room. You can watch what's happening from down there."

"But—"

He took her arm, gently ushering her toward the door. "No buts, Keira. Leo will kill me if anything happens to you."

She growled, but complied. "Fine. I know my way down there. You go stop them."

"Straight to the bunker, Keira. No detours."

She nodded and hurried out.

Ty turned to the rest of them just as the front door banged closed.

Clary's heart jumped into her throat and she turned fearful eyes toward the front of the house.

"Ty? Keira?"

Clary recognized Leo's voice.

"In the security room!" Ty yelled down the hall.

Leo appeared in the doorway a moment later, his eyes scanning the group congregated there. He frowned fiercely.

"Where's Keira?"

"I already sent her to the safe room. Phobos and Deimos crossed the wall along the back of the property."

Leo stepped forward to fiddle with the security system. "Where are they now?"

"I don't know. They tripped a sensor on the back perimeter and now nothing."

Leo typed in some commands, and the monitors on the wall went back to their full configuration. He rewound the footage from the time the alarm tripped, then stepped back.

"What's he doing?" Clary whispered to Colin.

"He's going to watch the feeds and try to pick up the twins' trail once they scaled the wall."

"How? You can't see them. They're like the wind."

"Super-sight, remember?"

Clary stared at the back of Leo's head, dumbfounded. "I did not realize that applied to film."

Leo pressed play on the remote and the images on the screens began to move. Clary stood, silent, while he watched the screens. He fast-forwarded momentarily, then zoomed in on one screen, freezing an image. A man with long black hair stood next to a building, staring out.

"There's one. Near the stable, watching the house." He hit play again, pausing a moment later on an identical man in the garden.

"The one by the stable will see us coming," Colin said. "There's no cover between the house and the stable except for a couple of trees."

Leo pulled his cell from his pocket and hit a number in his favorites. Keira's face immediately popped onto the screen.

"Leo!"

"Hey, *chère*. We need a bubble. We've got one god hunkered down at the edge of the stable. The other's in the garden."

"I'll do my best. Junior's awake and doing somersaults. Can you come fiddle with this monitor in here so I can see what's going on? I have no idea how to work any of this crap."

He rolled his eyes. "I showed you how."

She stared back at him and just blinked.

He sighed and Clary bit back a smile. They were cute. "Fine. I'll be there in a sec."

He hung up and turned to Clary. "Doc, you're coming with me. It's safer if you stay in the bunker with Keira."

Clary nodded, not about to argue. Her special abilities rested in her brain, not her brawn. She was perfectly content to stay out of the way.

Laying a hand on Colin's arm, she caught his gaze. "Be careful."

He nodded and laid a hand over hers, giving it a gentle squeeze.

With one last look, Clary followed Leo from the room.

CHAPTER 13

"What's the plan, Leo?" Colin asked. He and the others were gathered just inside the backdoor. After Leo took Clary to the safe room, he returned to the security room with a vial and a box full of the comm units he brought back from his house.

"We're going after the one in the garden first. Can you blind him when we get close?" Leo asked. "If I can get my arms around him, Ty and Luca can get Keira's sleepy-juice in him." He held up the vial. "Then we can take him back to the house, where she can put something around him to hold him until Hades can come get him." He held up the vial.

Colin nodded, adjusting the earpiece to his comm unit. "Just know that I won't be of much help if he fights back. It's going to take most of my concentration to hold the darkness on such a small and strong target."

"Got it. Let's go."

They filed out the door and paused at the edge of the patio behind the pergola's pillars. Rain soaked their clothes almost immediately. Lightning flashed and thunder boomed. Colin couldn't help but wonder how much of the storm was natural and what the gods were causing.

Leo hit the button on his comm mic. "*Chère*, we're ready."

Colin felt energy crackle around them, even though he saw nothing.

"Let's move," Leo breathed.

Silently, the five of them crept toward the garden, using the curtain of rain as cover. Colin felt a little strange, not having a gun in his hands while advancing on a target. It wouldn't do any good, since the bad guy was immortal.

Because of Keira's energy bubble, they crossed the lawn quickly. Stepping lightly, they entered the garden, keeping to the hedges as they crept toward the center where they last saw the god on the camera feed. Colin peered around the hedge to see him looking to the heavens, eyes glowing silver. The god's head whipped toward them, a frown creasing his brow, but he didn't move. Lightning crackled overhead, and thunder rolled, reverberating through Colin's chest.

He held his breath as the god looked right at him. His heart thundered in his ears. He was sure Keira's bubble had failed and they had been discovered. After a moment, the god turned back to the house.

Leo crept to within feet of the god before he gestured around him. Colin figured he was indicating the bubble only he could see. It must extend out several feet from them.

Gathering his concentration, Colin looked inward, gathering his ability.

Leo gave him a nod, and Colin plunged the god into complete darkness.

Immediately, the god stiffened and his eyes went wide. Clouds gathered overhead and more lightning cracked through the sky.

"You cannot stop me!"

A sense of fear swept over Colin. He sucked in a breath, struggling against the wave to hold his concentration. This must be Phobos. He tried not to panic, reminding himself it was all an illusion, as the feeling that they were all about to die took hold. It was a trick of the mind. It didn't make him any less scared, but it helped to ground him and give him the courage to continue.

Leo took two large steps forward and wrapped him up in a bearhug.

Leaves swirled as the storm intensified and the wind kicked up. Energy swirled around them, making all the hair on Colin's arms stand on end. Lightning shot out of the sky to land only yards away. He fought to hold the darkness, drawing on his Special Forces training to keep his concentration. Phobos couldn't hit what he couldn't see.

"Keira, you can drop the bubble," Penny said into her mic. She stayed near Colin, shielding him from harm while he kept the god in the dark. "Do we know where the other one is?"

"Still at the barn, but he's looking your way," Clary said.

Lightning bolts rained down around them. Colin cursed, willing his panic back into its box and held the darkness, praying he didn't get struck.

"Ty! Luca! Do it now!" Leo yelled over the roar of thunder.

The two men ran forward. Ty attempted to force the god's mouth open, but it was clamped tight.

The wind increased as the core of the storm reached them. Colin spread his feet to stay upright. Branches creaked as they swayed. Thunder boomed. A leaf slapped him in the face, but he ignored it, concentrating on holding the god in the dark. He was strong and pushed against the darkness, trying to find a way around it.

"The other one's coming!" Clary yelled in his ear.

Phobos kicked out, sending Ty flying. He collided with Colin, sending them both crashing to the ground and breaking his concentration.

Colin rolled and bounced back to his feet, spinning around to see the god grab hold of Leo's arm and flip him over his head. Leo sprawled on his back in the dirt before quickly scrabbling back to his feet.

Deimos appeared at his twin's side, doubling the feeling of fear and dread weighing down on them all. Penny shrieked and backpedaled. Luca followed her. Ty, Leo, and Colin formed a line and faced the gods head-on.

Another lightning bolt streaked out of the sky. It crashed into the energy shield over their heads, popping and fizzling as it traveled over it to scorch the ground around them. Phobos roared and moved toward Colin, an evil smile on his face. Rain poured down out of the sky now, soaking them all.

Leo ran at him, but didn't make it far. Phobos yanked a small branch off a nearby tree and hurled it at him, impaling him in the side. Leo cried out and fell to his knees.

Ty ran to help him, while Colin stood his ground, attempting to impose the darkness on both gods. Every time he tried, though, lightning crashed down, barely missing him. He was having enough of an effect to throw off their aim.

"Where is Dr. Moncrief?" Deimos asked, his voice rumbled like the thunder booming overhead.

"Safe," Colin replied, anger burning in his chest. "You'll have to go through all of us to get to her."

Deimos's evil smile deepened. "That can be arranged." Dread hit Colin hard as the god ran forward, momentarily paralyzing Colin and giving Deimos an opportunity to catch him off-balance and knock him down. They rolled across the ground. Mud caked their bodies, making them slick. Colin slid through Deimos's grasp.

"I will kill you and your lovely friend and then no one will be able to stop us." Deimos rose, preparing to attack again.

Colin's anger soared, and his hands caught fire.

Deimos paused in his advance to stare at him.

Colin took advantage of his moment of surprise and sent the flames shooting toward the god. He dodged it, but Colin kept up a steady barrage, keeping him occupied while Leo and Phobos played tag.

One of his fireballs caught the wave of the god's hair as he spun away, setting it alight. Deimos paused in his forward motion to smack at the flames. Colin saw Luca square his shoulders and push forward against the fear and dread still permeating the air. Rain gathered in his hands, shaping into daggers and hardening to ice. Colin sent another wave of fire at Deimos to keep his attention. Luca ran up behind Deimos and swung, striking the god between the shoulder blades.

He roared in pain and stumbled forward, but didn't lose his footing. Colin sent more fire through the rain, keeping him off-balance. Luca swung again, but missed this time. Penny came at him from the other side as a mountain lion. She swiped at his chest, but he moved out of her way.

Colin heard the growl of a large cat and glanced over to see Ty leap at Phobos as a tiger just as Leo surged up from the ground, the branch that impaled him now in his hands. He used it like a spear and drove it at the god, but missed as Phobos sidestepped. Ty stayed with him, and landed his enormous paws on his chest, knocking him to the ground. Leo let out a determined yell, running forward with his spear, blood soaking the side of his shirt. He let loose the branch, sending it through Phobos's abdomen, bringing him to his knees.

Deimos, sensing his twin's distress, turned, giving Colin the opening he needed. He landed a fireball in the god's gut, knocking him back. Penny landed on his back, biting into his neck while Luca gathered the rain pouring out of the sky and funneled it at the god's face, up his nose and down his throat.

"Where's the sleep potion?" Colin asked.

Ty returned to his human form and felt his pockets, cursing when he reached in and pulled out two broken vials.

In a surge of power, Deimos pushed up from the onslaught of rain, backing away, then moving to Phobos's side. He straightened, his brother in his arms, and looked at the five of them. Hesitation crossed his face for the first time.

Before any of them could react, he ran at Penny. Knocking her down, he fled past her, carrying his twin, toward the rear of the property.

Leo tapped his mic. "*Chère*, look at the feeds on the backside of the grounds. Do you see him?"

"One of the cameras shifted again," Keira said after a momentary pause. "It looks like they hopped the wall and left."

"Copy. We're headed in."

They ran back to the house. Shoes squeaking, they climbed the steps to the porch and filed inside to the mudroom. Water puddled at their feet. Colin edged his shoes off and was in the process of peeling off his socks when footsteps sounded in the hall outside the kitchen. Keira and Clary quickly appeared, stopping in the doorway to the mudroom.

Keira's eyes widened as she noticed the blood running down Leo's right side. She ran forward.

"Oh my God, Leo! What happened?"

"He flung a branch at me. Ty pulled it out. It didn't go that deep. The rain made it look worse than it is, *chère*. A few stitches and I'll be fine."

"Are you sure?" Her hand shook as she cupped his jaw, forcing him to look down at her. He covered her hand with his, a tender look in his eyes.

"I'm fine. I promise."

Heedless of his soaked clothes, she stood on tiptoe and kissed him fiercely.

Clary cleared her throat. "I'll go get you all some towels." She glanced at Colin through her lashes, her eyes roving over the shirt molded to his chest, then spun on her heel and hurried away.

Ty whipped his shirt off and tossed it in the industrial sink against the kitchen wall. His socks followed it with a wet plop. Luca, who hadn't had a chance to do more than take off his suit coat before the alarm blared, loosened his tie and began unbuttoning his dress shirt.

Eager to shed his own sopping wet clothes, Colin yanked his shirt over his head just as Clary reentered the kitchen, a stack of towels in her arms.

CHAPTER 14

Clary's step faltered momentarily as she entered the kitchen.

Sweet Jesus.

Colin stood just inside the mudroom, naked from the waist up. Her eyes roved over his muscled chest and lower.

He took a towel off her stack, muscles rippling with the movement, and passed it back to Penny, who took it with a grateful smile and began wringing the water out of her soaked shirt and hair.

Clary felt her cheeks heat and resisted the urge to fan herself. She had been right about those rock-hard washboard abs.

What she hadn't expected was the full-sleeve tattoo on his left arm or the words inked over the right side of his ribcage. Unabashedly, she studied the intricate design on his arm while he dried himself off. Clary loved tattoos and had several of her own on various parts of her body. She loved them. Her tattoo artist had done a fantastic job.

Colin's, though, were on an entirely different level. It was like looking at a charcoal drawing done by da Vinci. At the top of his arm, a flag fluttered in an unseen breeze. It faded into a series of crosses, each bearing a name and date. A patch she assumed belonged to his military unit sat beneath those connected by swirling bands of steel. On his forearm, an anvil sat atop a stone, a hand holding a blacksmith's hammer striking the piece of metal resting on it. Sparks shot out in all directions. It was like someone had taken a photograph of the moment, it was so lifelike.

Her eyes traveled back up his arm and across his chest to the words emblazoned on his ribs. She couldn't make them out because they wrapped around his side, but it looked like some kind of creed.

When she finally met his gaze again, a knowing smile sat on his sculpted lips. Clary felt her cheeks heat, but she didn't look away. Couldn't.

It wasn't until Penny spoke that Clary remembered where they were and what caused him to be shirtless.

"I'm going to go change," Penny said, moving toward the kitchen.

"Yeah," Ty said, agreeing. "Once we're all dry, we need to search Henley's boat. Hopefully, he'll be there and we can get some insight into Phobos and Deimos's plans before they can devise another strategy to get to Clary."

Clary jolted at her name, the fog of lust finally dissipating. Her eyes shot to Ty. "What? They were after me? Why?"

"They didn't say, but they were real interested in where you are."

Colin reached out and brushed her cheek with the tips of his fingers. "Maybe you should stay here with Leo and Keira."

Sensation zinged through her skin at the feel of his touch. She did her best to ignore it and focus on the conversation.

"No. If they want me dead, the last place I want to be is anywhere near Keira. Leo would be our only defense. As well as he can fight, he still has to fight like he can die. Phobos and Deimos don't. It's going to take more than one of you to bring them down."

Leo laid a hand over Colin's shoulder. "She's right. I hate to admit it, but now that we know she has a target on her back from the twins and not just Henley, it's safer for all of us if she stays with you."

Colin looked back at him and finally nodded. "Let's all go get dry. We need to move if we're going to catch up with Dr. Henley."

The group filed out around Clary except for Colin. He stood in front of her in all his half-naked glory.

She clenched her hands together to keep from reaching out and running them over his hair-roughened, tattooed chest. He, though, had no such qualms about touching her. He wove a hand through the loosening strands of her ponytail on the side of her head, cupping her jaw. Clary's resolve wavered. She clenched her hands tighter, her knuckles turning white. If she touched him, she was going to end up climbing him like a tree.

"I won't let him anywhere near you. He'll have to go through me—and all the others—first," he said, misinterpreting her behavior as fear.

"I know," she breathed. Caught in his aqua eyes, she leaned closer. Without her consent, her hands unclenched and lightly skimmed his abs.

He sucked in a breath at her touch, the muscles jumping beneath her fingers. His pupils went dark and his free hand snaked out to circle her waist. He tugged her against his body. Clary slid her hands up his chest to curl over the tops of his shoulders. The hand cupping her jaw tipped her head back, and his thumb traced her bottom lip.

The breath caught in Clary's chest at the intensity in his eyes as he stared down at her. He needed to kiss her before she died of oxygen deprivation.

When he finally leaned in and sealed his mouth to hers, it was like someone pressed play. She inhaled deeply, filling her nose with his earthy scent. Her body lit up like the Christmas tree in the living room and she clutched at his shoulders. She was thankful for his arm around her, because her knees had turned to jelly.

His tongue swept past her lips and she moaned at the taste of him, which only spurred him on. The hand around her waist drifted south to curve around her butt. He squeezed and her belly clenched with need. He had barely touched her and this was already the best kiss she'd ever had.

She speared her fingers into his hair and wiggled closer. A deep moan rumbled up his chest and skated down her nerve endings to ratchet up her need. The desire to wrap her legs around his waist hit her hard, and she knew they needed to stop now. The mudroom in the midst of a crisis was not the time or place for this.

Abruptly, she ripped her mouth from his and stared up at him, chest heaving.

"You should go change," she managed to say.

A sexy grin spread across his handsome face. "Probably. I can wait, though." He squeezed her butt again, and she bit her lip, holding in the moan.

"Yes, but time is critical."

That big hand caressed her jaw once more, his gaze intense. He placed a soft, lingering kiss on her lips. A touch so tender it made Clary's heart flutter. She could so very easily fall in love with this man.

He raised his head, brushing his thumb over her cheek once more, then let her go.

"I'm going to get dry. But we're putting a pin in this to revisit later."

She nodded, and he walked past her into the kitchen.

Clary spun around, watching him leave. She clamped her lips together to hold in the whimper at the sight of his broad back retreating. His muscles shifted, fluid under his golden skin as he moved. His wet jeans molded to his butt and thighs, promising that there was more of the same beneath the fabric.

She braced a hand on the doorway and took a deep breath through her nose, silently berating herself as he disappeared around the corner.

There are deranged, ancient Greek gods after you, and your research partner wants to hypnotize the world into starting a war. Get a grip, Clary!

Closing her eyes briefly, she shoved thoughts of Colin and all his muscles and beautiful tattoos from her mind and walked out of the mudroom. It was time to focus.

CHAPTER 15

"The boat's dark." Colin let up on his throat mic after relaying the information to Ty, Penny, and Luca. They were in the water, waiting on his word to board the ship.

"Maybe he's sleeping," Clary said from beside him.

"Could be. It feels empty, though. There aren't any chairs on the deck or towels hanging. Look at the other boats. You can tell which ones are occupied." He pointed down the dock.

"How can you see anything? All I see are outlines."

He grinned. "God of darkness, remember?" He could always see well in the dark, but now it was like having a lantern over everything. This would have come in handy so many times over the years.

She rolled her eyes. "Y'all have cool stuff. What do I get? The ability to lucid dream. I feel gypped."

"Don't. That's all you know about. Have you tried to access anything else?"

"Not really, no."

"Why not?"

"Honestly? Partly because things have been so busy and partly because the whole thing scares me. It still doesn't feel real."

He grunted. "I get that. But it is. Nothing to do but accept it and move on."

"I'm trying."

"Good." He took her hand. "Come on. Let's go see if anyone's home." Keeping Clary tucked close, he headed for the darkened boat. She could be right and Henley was sleeping, but he didn't think so. The place felt abandoned.

Stopping on the dock next to the gleaming white yacht, he motioned for her to stay put, then ran the length of the slip, looking through windows, but seeing nothing.

"It's clear," he said into his mic.

A slight splash was the only response before he saw Ty roll over the bow. Luca followed him while Penny popped up over the stern. She helped Clary on board while he jumped on close to the bridge.

Before they left the estate, they'd discussed what they would do once they got here. Penny and Clary were staying topside as lookouts while Colin, Ty, and Luca searched below.

Using hand signals, Ty motioned for the women to duck low and keep an eye out, then Colin led the way inside. He drew his weapon as they filed through the door. It wouldn't do squat against the gods who attacked them earlier, but it would stop Dr. Henley just fine. With his increased night vision, they moved swiftly through to the main cabin and down the hallway leading to several bedrooms. As they searched, he couldn't help but wonder who was bankrolling Henley's operation. This was some boat.

They reached the end of the hall and the main suite. The door stood open to the empty room.

"Dammit," Luca muttered.

Colin hung his head. "It's clear."

"Penny, you and Clary can come down," Ty said into his mic.

"Let's go back to the main living area," Colin said, motioning them back the way they came. They turned and headed down the hall, entering the living room as Penny and Clary came down the stairs.

"Anything?" Penny asked.

Ty shook his head. "Nope. If he was here, he's gone now. The bed was made and everything, so he didn't just run out for a bit."

"Fan out and search. Maybe we'll get lucky and find something that tells us where he went."

Clary snorted. "I doubt it. And if we do find something, it'll probably be a plant like the cylinder in my office."

"We still need to look," Luca said.

Clapping filled the room. They jumped and glanced around, looking for the source. Colin's eyes landed on the intercom.

"I thought about letting you search, but decided I was bored with this game."

"Brandon," Clary said, honing in on the speaker. "What are you doing? This is insane!"

"Is it? Have you seen what's happening in the world, Clary? The pettiness amongst humans. The selfishness. The lack of caring about anything except the almighty dollar?" He scoffed. "It's time for a reset. For the weak and the ungrateful to die, so a stronger, better human race can rise. So *we* can rise."

"Dude, you sound like the guy from X-Men," Ty said. "Just because we have special abilities doesn't make us better people than someone who doesn't."

"You are entitled to your opinion, detective, even if it's wrong. I'm not calling to debate, though."

"Why are you calling?" Clary asked. "To gloat that you're still one step ahead of us?" Anger tinged her voice. She wished he was here so she could strangle him herself.

"No. I'm calling to say goodbye. You see, there's a bomb on the ship that was activated the moment you stepped on board."

Colin's eyes widened, and a gasp went through the room.

"I'd say you've got, oh, a minute and a half to get clear. It won't matter, though. There's enough radiation in it to make people sick for several city blocks. The war has begun. I just wish you all could be around to see us victorious." The intercom clicked as he hung up, then went silent.

Curses flew through the room, but Colin ignored them all. His mind spun with a floor plan of the yacht. "Everyone quiet!" All eyes turned to him. "The bomb will be above the waterline to have that large of a dispersal radius. And it will be large. Fan out. Holler for me if you find it."

They all ran in different directions. Luca went for the bar, and Penny for the living room furniture. Colin, Ty, and Clary ran up the stairs to check the bridge and deck.

"I've got the supply room," Luca said.

Colin nodded and pointed Clary toward the deck seats. "Check those. I'll get the bridge." He didn't wait for her to respond, running up the stairs to the wheelhouse instead. He yanked off the panel under the wheel, but was greeted by a mess of normal boat wiring. He crouched and shone his flashlight inside, just to be sure, but saw nothing out of the ordinary.

Standing, he perused the rest of the small cabin, his eyes landing on the seats. They were just big enough to house something like that. He dug his knife from his pocket and flipped it open, slicing into the leather on the captain's chair. A blinking red light flashed, bright in the darkness.

He touched his mic. "Guys, I found it. Wheelhouse." He put his light between his teeth and pulled the leather away from the bomb. There were forty seconds left on the device.

Sweat popped out on his brow as he studied the wiring, trying to ignore the timer. Footsteps pounded up the stairs, echoing his heartbeat in his ears.

"Shit!" Ty's curse cut through the pounding. "There's only twenty seconds left. Maybe we can survive if we jump in the water and dive deep enough."

Colin grunted around his light but didn't stop tracing wires. The marina was too shallow for this amount of explosives. His mind put together a blueprint as he studied it, routing circuits and flashing danger zones.

The timer ticked to five seconds.

"Sweet Jesus," Ty breathed.

He heard Ty shuffle toward Penny. Clary's hand landed on his back, and he heard her hiccup as she tried to suppress her emotions.

The plans clicked into place. He grabbed a wire and yanked. The clock froze at two seconds.

"Oh my God!" Penny cried.

Ty laughed. "Oh, yeah! Take that, assholes!"

"Wow, that was close." Luca blew out a breath.

Colin turned and looked up at Clary, who still had her hand on his shoulder. She smiled down at him.

"You did it."

He stood, running a hand up her arm. "I couldn't let him win. It would have been too easy."

She laughed—loud, body-shaking laughs—then threw her arms around him. He cradled her close, relief and the adrenaline dump making his limbs shake.

"How did you know which wire to pull?" Luca stepped closer to get a better look at the bomb.

"Experience."

Ty snorted. "And a little special talent."

"Well, regardless, we're alive, and I appreciate that," Luca said.

"Trust me, I'm glad I can do what I can, too. Let's get this thing disassembled and get it out of here. Maybe we can learn more about what they're planning."

"Didn't Henley say there's nuclear material in there?" Ty said.

"It's shielded," Colin said. "Probably to protect the bomber."

"Did Henley plant it?"

"I doubt it," Clary said. "He's not very mechanically inclined."

"So, who's his accomplice, then?" Penny said.

"Someone with explosive experience," Colin said. "A cop, maybe. Or ex-military."

"You're sure?" Luca said.

Colin nodded. "Yeah. That's a sophisticated device. The only reason I was able to defuse it is because they weren't counting on anyone finding it to do that. That won't be the case if they do this again."

"Agreed," Ty said. "All right. Let's get moving. I don't want to be here when the fishermen show up in a few hours."

Over the next hour, they worked to get the chair off the boat as well as search. Colin ran to bring his car closer, while Penny and Clary looked for tools to unbolt the chair from the floor. Luca and Ty searched the cabin and wheelhouse for evidence while Colin took care of the bomb. Once it was free of the floor, Ty carried it out to the waiting vehicle.

"I can't say I'm eager to ride home with a nuke, but let's get out of here." Clary opened the passenger door to get in.

Colin held up a hand. "Wait. You're not riding with me. No one is."

"What?" She frowned over the hood at him.

"It's too dangerous. Penny's SUV is just down the dock. You can ride with them."

"He's right, Clary," Ty said. "If something goes wrong, it's better if only one of us is taken out in the blast."

She huffed and slammed the car door. "Why does it have to be you?" She waved a hand. "Not that I'm wishing anyone else dead."

"We get it. But Colin's the most qualified. He knows explosives. How to handle them. He'll be fine." Ty put a hand on her shoulder.

Her frown deepened, but she backed away with him. "Fine." She looked at him. Her pretty blue eyes pierced him, even in the darkness. "Please be careful."

"I will. You too." Tearing his eyes from hers, he opened his door and climbed inside. He wished she could ride with him. It bothered him to let her out of his sight, but it was safer for her if she didn't. The bomb was stable, but he wasn't taking any chances.

He turned the engine over and pulled away from the dock, casting one last glance in the mirror to watch her walk away before forcing his attention to the task at hand. Pulling out of the marina, he kept a steady pace back to Ty and Penny's, doing his best not to hit pot holes or take turns too sharp.

Half an hour after he set out, he pulled into the driveway. After entering the code to get onto the property, he pulled up to the front door and cut the engine, heaving a deep sigh that at least that part of this mission was done.

Leo came outside as Colin got out of the car.

"Ty called. You really defused a suitcase bomb with two seconds to spare?"

Colin nodded. "It's a chair bomb, though." He opened the back hatch on his jeep to show him the wingback chair they removed from the yacht.

"Damn. Let's get it in the garage. We need to figure out what we're going to do with all this nuclear material." He reached in and grabbed the chair.

"Maybe Luca will know what to do with it. He's a fed. They have to have a plan for this."

Leo hefted the chair over his head. "Yeah, but that's through official channels. We can't turn this over to those."

"No, definitely not. Dude, doesn't your side hurt?" Colin walked ahead to open the garage door.

"Some. Not enough to slow me down, though. For an all-powerful being, he's got terrible aim. It only pierced the muscle layer. A few stitches and one of Keira's potions, and I'm fine." Leo followed him inside, then set the chair by the workbench.

"Is it safe?" Keira peered through the doorway from the kitchen.

"Stay there, *chère*. We don't want to take any chances."

"He's right," Colin said. "It's shielded, but it could still leak low levels of radiation."

She nodded. "How about you two come over here, too, then?"

Colin wasn't about to argue with her. He was ready to be out of the device's presence. The three of them filed inside as another of the garage doors rose. Ty pulled in and shut the car off.

"Luca has a plan," Ty said as they climbed out.

"Good," Leo said from the doorway. "Let's go in the living room and hear it."

They followed him through the house and dropped into chairs. Fatigue hit Colin as he settled onto the sofa with Clary by his side.

He'd been riding the adrenaline all the way home, but now that they were safe, the late hour and stress were getting to him.

"So, what's your plan?" Leo asked once everyone was settled.

"I think we all agree we need to know what kind of nuclear material they're using, right?"

Several heads bobbed, including Colin's.

"I know a guy who can test it for us. He's one of us, but he works for a university lab. They do testing on radioactive isotopes on a fairly regular basis, so it won't throw up any alarm bells if he uses the equipment. If we can figure out where they're getting the material, we might be able to figure out where they are and who else is involved."

"Question." Keira held up a finger. "You keep saying one of us and hinting that there are more like us. How many, exactly?"

Luca shrugged. "I know a dozen or so, personally, not including you guys." He held up a hand. "But that's a rarity. I only know so many because of my mother. Many people who know what they are, know of my family in some way." He shrugged. "I don't know why or how that works. It just is. It has something to do with her abilities as a psychic. She seeks some families out, but others find their way to her. Sometimes, that's because one of the gods comes down—like Athena—and guides them to her."

"Do you think she can give us any insights into what's going on or where Henley and his friends are hiding out?" Colin asked.

"Maybe. I'm involved, so I'm not sure how much she'll be able to see. It's worth a shot, though. Even if she can't give us anything but vague ideas and riddles, it's at least a place to start."

"Yeah," Penny said. "It's more than we have now."

"Okay," Leo said. "Let's all get some sleep. We'll get the chair and cylinder to Luca's friend and talk to his mother first thing tomorrow." He rose and held a hand out to Keira to help her up.

Colin pushed to his feet, Clary rising beside him. She stifled a yawn. "Sleep sounds wonderful," she said.

He agreed.

"I'm glad we bought beds the other day," Penny said. "And that we filled all the rooms and not just two for Colin and Clary." She smiled at Luca.

Ty grinned. "Let's just not pick up any more strays. We're out of space."

She laughed. "And here I thought this house was too big."

"We'll hopefully be out of your hair soon, and things can go back to normal," Luca said.

"Normal would be nice," Penny said. She headed for the door. "Come on. Ty and I will show you to your room. It's just past ours."

The rest of them followed her up the stairs to their own rooms. Colin offered Clary a soft smile as he ducked into his room. He closed the door and let out a breath, letting the quiet soak in. Stripping out of his clothes, he went into the attached bath and turned on the shower. He let the water warm a moment before stepping into the spray.

The hot water stung, but he savored the pain. It reminded him he was alive. He came close to not being that way. He still could hardly believe what he'd done tonight. What was waiting in the garage for Luca to take to his friend. His life had become rather surreal in the last few days.

Colin lingered in the shower, only stepping out when the water turned chilly. He grabbed a towel from the rack on the wall and wiped the water from his body, then tossed it in the hamper and walked back into the bedroom. After flipping off the light, he pulled the covers back and climbed into bed.

He no more than shut his eyes than a loud thump came from Clary's room next door. Curses carried through the wall. He couldn't make out what she said, but from her tone, they were likely colorful.

Heaving a sigh, Colin got out of bed and located a pair of sweats, not bothering with underwear. Once he checked on her and made sure she was okay, he was coming straight back here, stripping once again, and passing out for the next few hours.

He tugged open his door and walked the few feet to hers, knocking softly. "Clary? Are you okay?"

"I'm fine. Just dropped something." Her voice wobbled, making Colin frown.

"Are you sure? You don't sound okay. Open the door."

"I'm fine, really."

"I'm sure you are, but I just want to see you to be certain. Too many weird things have happened for me to go on blind faith." Silence met his words. He waited, giving her a moment to get to the door.

It cracked open, and she peered through. "See? I'm fine." Her eyes went wide as she took in his appearance.

Colin's skin heated as her gaze roved over him from head to toe, lingering on his torso before snapping up to stare at his neck. He swallowed hard and willed his body to behave. "You're not fine. You've been crying." Tear tracks stained her cheeks, and the eyes that perused him only moments before were red-rimmed.

She sniffed and still refused to look him in the eye. "I'm fine."

"So you've said. What's wrong?"

Her eyes shot to his, and her brow furrowed. "You have to ask that question?"

His mouth flattened. "Okay. What part of what's happened has you so upset?"

She looked at his neck again. "All of it. Mostly, I'm just mourning the loss of my normal life."

"Well, hopefully we'll all get back to our lives soon."

She snorted. "Nothing will ever be normal again."

He smiled. "No. But we can make a new normal."

She nodded, sniffing again.

Colin reached out and wiped away a tear track with his thumb. "Do you want me to sit with you for a while?"

Her eyes widened a moment, straying to his naked chest, before she schooled her expression and shook her head. "No. I'm okay now. I just want to go to sleep."

He nudged her chin up to make her look at him, then held her gaze. Her pretty blue eyes shimmered with emotion, but he could see she had it under control now. "Okay. I'll let you get to bed. Just bang on the wall if you need anything." A wrinkle creased his forehead. "Or drop whatever you did again."

She smiled. "It was my suitcase. I moved it off the bed to the chair, and I missed." She opened the door wider so he could see the mess of clothes on the floor by the chair.

"Do you want some help picking all that up?"

She shook her head. "No. I've got it. I might just leave it until morning." She shrugged.

"All right. Well, goodnight."

"Goodnight."

He turned away to head back to his room.

"Colin?"

He looked back.

"Thank you for checking on me."

He offered her another smile. "You're welcome. See you in the morning."

She echoed his smile and stepped back, closing the door.

CHAPTER 16

Clary leaned her forehead against the door and blew out a breath. Why did she have to drop her suitcase? She could have had her cry and crawled into bed with no one the wiser. Now, she had gritty eyes and the image of Colin's perfect chest stamped into her brain. And a desire to see what was beneath those sweats. She was pretty sure he hadn't been wearing underwear.

She pushed away from the door with a huff and turned off the light, heading for bed. At least she had a chance at decent dreams tonight. He might star front and center in them instead of nightmares about being blown to smithereens by a nuke.

Adjusting her pillows, Clary closed her eyes and forced her mind to clear, doing a deep breathing exercise she learned years ago in medical school to help her get to sleep when she only had time for a quick nap. In minutes, she dropped off.

It wasn't long before she woke in a dream. She was back in the creepy forest again.

So much for Colin wiping away my nightmares. Clary sighed.

"Hello? Is anyone out there?"

"Help me."

Clary shrieked and spun around at the sound of the voice directly behind her. The woman from the other dream stood there, her amber eyes locked on Clary.

"Who are you? I need to know who you are to help you." She blinked, and when she opened her eyes, she stood in the strangely beautiful field, looking at the black castle in the distance.

"Help me." The words were whispered in her ear, but the woman was gone.

Clary spun a full circle. "Dammit. Where did she go?" She walked forward, but only took two steps before the scene morphed back to her bedroom at Ty and Penny's. Before she could wonder why she was back here, there was a knock on the door.

She answered it, not knowing what to expect on the other side. She pulled the door open and came face to face with Colin's naked chest once again.

"Are you okay?"

Was she reliving their encounter earlier? Maybe wishing for a different ending?

She gave a mental shrug. Why not? It was just a dream. And it would help wipe away the memory of that bizarre-looking woman and her pleas for help.

"I'm fine. Just a bad dream." She stepped forward, reaching out to run a finger along the waistband of his sweats. Immediately, he swelled beneath the fabric.

"Clary?" The question in his voice was crystal clear.

One corner of her mouth rose in a coy smile. "Come help me forget?"

Heat licked his eyes, and he stepped inside, kicking the door shut. His hands cupped her jaw, those long fingers tunneling into her hair. He stared at her for a moment before his mouth crashed onto hers.

Clary moaned and sagged into him. She could feel him against her stomach, hot and hard through his sweats. Moisture pooled between her legs as she got a better idea of what was hiding behind the charcoal gray fabric.

His big hands cupped her butt and lifted her. Holding her snug to his body, he walked toward her bed and tossed her on it. She bounced once, then he was on her, his mouth attacking hers while his long fingers roved over her skin. Clary shivered beneath his touch. She'd had a handful of sex dreams, but never any like this. She could feel her body grow more aroused with each stroke of his hands on her flesh. Colin was going to give her the best orgasm of her life without ever laying an actual finger on her.

Her clothing disappeared as he whisked it off her body. Clary slid her hands inside the waist of his sweats and pushed them down, freeing his erection. She filled her hands with his hot length and squeezed.

Colin groaned and thrust into her hands. "You keep that up and this is going to end before it starts."

She grinned. "Nah. I think we'll be good." It was her dream, after all. She could do whatever she wanted.

Feeling naughtier by the second, Clary squeezed again and stroked her hand down his shaft. When he moaned and his eyelids fluttered, she took advantage of his momentary distraction and pushed on his chest, flipping them over to straddle him.

He smiled up at her. "Who said you get to be on top?"

"Me."

He shrugged and reached for her breasts. "Fine by me. Puts these in easy touching distance." He cupped the heavy globes in his palms and teased the tips.

Clary's core pulsed, and she moaned. "I'd say we take our time, but I don't want to." She lifted her hips and moved higher up his body until he slid beneath her.

Colin rolled his hips, rubbing against her sensitive flesh. "Me either. We can go slow next time."

She gave him a jerky nod and rose to her knees, grasping him in her hand. Lining him up with her entrance, she sank onto him, letting out a high-pitched sigh as he filled her. She adjusted her seat on him, letting her body get accustomed to his size. It didn't take long before she couldn't sit still. She needed to move. Needed to feel him stroke her walls. Clary put her hands on his chest and lifted her hips.

They both moaned. He grasped her waist and pushed her down as he rose up. Clary saw stars at the exquisite sensation.

"Faster," she breathed and rolled her hips.

She didn't have to tell him twice. He tightened his grip on her waist and held her steady above him as he quickened his pace. Clary soared over the edge with a shriek. She didn't have a chance to come down from her high before he flipped her over. On his knees, he put her feet on his shoulders and held her thighs, changing the angle of his thrusts. The waves of pleasure rolling through her grew into mountains again. She hit the crest and flew over the top, screaming his name.

Writhing on the bed, clutching the sheets, she didn't think she could take anymore, but her boneless, sated body wouldn't let her tell him so. He obviously wasn't finished, though, because he still thrust into her. Tendons stood out in his neck, and his abs flexed with each stroke. Clary became transfixed, watching the muscles contract and relax as he moved. Sweat slicked his skin, making the ink on his body shine.

The waves built once more. She whimpered as her climax grew, knowing this one would wreck her. He pushed her legs wider and leaned down to draw the tip of her breast into his mouth. His tongue flicked the budded nipple, then he bit down. Clary let out a squawk of surprise. Her core clenched.

Colin let go of her breast with a pop. He sucked in a harsh breath, thrusting harder, before he let out a growl, followed by a quick shout as his release finally gripped him. She felt him pulse inside her, and her own climax broke. She cried out as wave after wave of the most intense pleasure she'd ever known flowed over her like molten lava. The heat kept going. The waves building on themselves as he held her legs open, keeping her from quashing them. By the time the final shiver rolled down her spine, Clary was nothing more than a sad sack of a woman, unable to move. All the starch had left her body.

Oh, that was just what I needed to sleep well. Body sated and mind quiet from her earth-shaking orgasms from dream-Colin, Clary fell into a deep sleep.

CHAPTER 17

Colin stared out the window, not seeing the passing scenery as Luca drove him and Ty west toward Atlanta and his friend, who could identify what they were dealing with.

His mind wasn't on their task, though. He kept reliving the dream he had last night. In it, he went back to Clary's room, and she invited him in. What followed was nothing short of extraordinary. He woke to wet sheets and bone deep satisfaction. He couldn't shake how real it was. It was unlike any dream he'd ever had. So much so, he avoided Clary this morning. He went for a run when he woke up, then showered and grabbed coffee and breakfast before she emerged from her room. Then he hid out on the porch until Ty and Luca were ready to leave.

That couldn't last. He'd have to face her at some point. He needed time to process the dream, though. To deal with the intense emotions it provoked and file them away so he could be around her without betraying his thoughts. He had the next couple of days for that. They were staying overnight in Atlanta, so they didn't have to make the trip twice—once to drop off the cylinders and a second one to pick them up.

Luca exited the interstate and wove through the city streets to the outskirts of the business district in the Atlanta suburbs. He pulled into the parking lot of a large steel and glass structure, stopping at the guardhouse. He showed his credentials to the guard.

"We're here to see Dr. Foerster."

The guard passed a clipboard through the window. "Sign in, please."

Luca wrote their names down and handed it back.

"You can park in lot B. He's on the third floor."

"Thank you."

The guard nodded and raised the gate. Luca drove through and parked. The three of them got out, Colin carrying the case with the two canisters of radioactive material, and walked inside. They showed their badges to security at the front desk. The guard gave them each a visitor's badge, then directions to Dr. Forester's lab. They rode the elevator to the third floor and followed the signs for nuclear geophysics.

"He's in there." Luca pointed through a large window at a man hunched over a computer. He knocked on the glass.

The man looked up, then smiled when he recognized his visitor. He stood and walked to the door to let them in.

"Did you have any trouble finding me?"

Luca shook his head. "No. Matt, this is Ty Farris and Colin Jacobs. Ty, Colin, this is Dr. Matt Foerster."

"Call me Matt, please." They all shook hands, then he ushered them inside. "So, what did you bring me, Luca? You were rather cryptic on the phone."

Luca looked at Colin and motioned for him to give the case to Matt. Colin set it on the desk and opened it.

Matt's eyes widened as he took in the shiny cylinders inside. "Is that what I think it is?"

"If you mean, is it radioactive material, then yes," Colin said. "We don't know what kind, though. That's where you come in."

With a frown, Matt picked up a Geiger counter and ran the wand over the cylinders, making the machine crackle slightly. "Well, they're fairly well sealed." He set the unit down. "Where did you get this stuff?"

"One canister was in a friend's desk—to frame her—and the other was attached to a bomb used to try to blow us up," Luca said.

Matt blinked. "Whoa. Okay. I'd ask what's going on, but I don't really want to know. I'd like to be able to deny all knowledge of whatever plot you're caught up in."

Luca gave a curt nod. "That's fine. The fewer people involved, the better. Do you think you can get us results tomorrow?"

"That shouldn't be a problem. Do you just want to know what it is, or do you want to know where it came from too?"

"The latter."

His head bobbed. "Okay. I'll do my best to identify the source."

"Sounds good," Luca said. "And I think it goes without saying, but don't tell anyone what you're doing or who you're doing it for. A lot of lives depend on us finding where that stuff came from and who took it."

"Not a problem. I get the feeling whatever you're caught up in, there's more at play than your run-of-the-mill criminals. I'm happy to stay out of the way of—that."

"Trust me, we'd love to as well," Ty said. He held out a hand. "Thanks for your time."

Matt took it. "Of course. I'm always happy to help out a friend." He glanced at Luca. "Stay safe, yeah?"

"Always." He shook Matt's hand. "Thanks again."

After Colin offered a handshake, the three of them left as quickly as they came. They weren't keen to linger anywhere, especially here. He didn't think they were followed, but it paid to be cautious. He just hoped there wasn't any trouble at home while they were gone.

CHAPTER 18

Colors swirled all around as Clary floated in a void. Whispers surrounded her, but she couldn't make out any words. It felt more like emotions than speech.

She closed her eyes and waited for something to materialize, or for the dream to change setting. One of the two always happened when she was in a void. This was the first one with so many colors, though. Usually, they were black or white.

Reaching a hand out, she touched the rainbow of colors waving past her. Thoughts and emotions bombarded her. They were so happy and innocent. It felt like what she imagined a small child dreamed about. Clary smiled and enjoyed the sensation until it abruptly cut off, and she found herself in the creepy place again.

She groaned and tipped her head back to look at the strangely glowing sky. "Can I get a clue what this is about this time?" She sighed and looked down, only to shriek and jump back. The strange woman stood in front of her again. Clary covered her racing heart with her hand. "Okay. This is getting ridiculous. Who are you? What do you want from me?" She snorted and shook her head. "God, I'm having a conversation with a figment of my imagination."

The woman pointed across the open field to the castle in the distance. "Help me."

"I would if you would tell me who you are and why you need my help." She growled. This was dumb. Why did she keep having the same dream? She closed her eyes and pictured Colin, trying to force her mind onto something else. She'd much rather dream about him screwing her brains out than this strange woman with the two-toned skin and glowing amber eyes.

Clary opened one eye. The woman still stood in front of her. *Dammit.* She heaved a sigh and opened both eyes. "Fine. How about you show me what you need help with? Can you do that?"

The woman pointed at the castle again.

"You need to get to the castle? Okay, let's go." She stepped around the woman.

"Help me."

"Aargh!" She spun around. "I'm trying." The world around her whirled in a riot of colors, making her dizzy. She closed her eyes and grabbed her head. When she opened them again, she was back in the dark forest and the woman was gone.

"Help me." The voice echoed all around her.

Clary turned a full circle in the woods, but saw nothing except trees. What the hell? What was going on? She hated dreams like this. Usually, when she lucid dreamed, it was about something mundane—like her day—or something fun. She could always manipulate it, but anytime that woman showed up, Clary was the one being manipulated.

With a sigh, she started walking. Maybe if she explored a bit, she would find some answers. She just prayed there weren't any surprises waiting for her. It was creepy in here.

One foot after another, she walked, pausing every so often to look around. She kept hoping to catch a glimpse of a clearing, but nothing but dark, dense woods greeted her. When she tripped over a gnarled root, she decided maybe she should watch her footing instead of her surroundings. Eyes on the ground, she didn't notice the house until she realized the trees had thinned. The white stucco, single-story home sat nestled in the trees. It looked inviting, which was a stark contrast to its surroundings.

Clary hurried forward to peer in the window. The inside was a mess. Furniture laid tipped over and upside down, the curtains were in pools on the floor, and bits of broken vases and knick knacks littered the floor. The scary looking woman's face popped into her head. She wondered if this was where she came from.

She stepped to the door and twisted the knob. The world around her whirled again, and she found herself back in the colorful void.

"Oh, come on!" She stomped her foot and huffed. Color swirled around her, trying to lift her mood. Clary sighed and touched the strand closest to her. Some of her ire melted away, and a small smile touched her lips. It was impossible not to feel happier here with this rainbow of emotion. She let more of her frustration float away. Whatever answers she was supposed to find wouldn't reveal themselves tonight.

CHAPTER 19

"So, you've got yourself some interesting stuff." Matt Foerster perched on a stool at the worktable in the center of his lab. He motioned for them to sit down.

Colin pulled out a stool and sat next to Ty. Luca took up residence at the end of the table closest to Matt.

"Why do you say that?" Luca asked.

Matt passed out a set of papers to each of them. "Both cylinders contained tritium. The one from the bomb also contained a plutonium-239 slurry."

Colin looked up, startled. "That's weapons grade. You can't get that just anywhere."

"Right. And it matches that produced at the Hanford Site in Washington state."

"Washington?" Ty said. "That's a far cry from South Carolina." He looked at Colin and Luca. "How did it get here?"

"I might have the answer to that," Matt said. "The tritium matches that produced at Savannah River. It's possible the plutonium was sent there for disposal and whoever stole the tritium also stole the plutonium."

"That makes sense," Colin said.

"Yeah. So, now we need to figure out who Brandon Henley knows at Savannah River," Luca said.

"I have a friend who's good at digging up information on people," Colin said. "I'll give her a call and see what she can find out. I'll talk to Clary, too, when we get back."

"That sounds good," Luca said. He looked at Matt. "I really appreciate you doing this. We needed a lead and you've just given us a good one."

Matt's smile was grim. "I just hope you can stop whoever is behind this before it's too late. Savannah River handles massive amounts of radioactive material. There could be a lot of this stuff out there." He pushed the black case they brought the cylinders in over to Luca. "Take care of that. And get it back into proper hands once you've apprehended your bad guy."

Luca picked up the case and stood. "Will do." He glanced at the others. "Let's get back to Charleston. We've got a lot to do."

CHAPTER 20

C lary stared up at the two-story white colonial house Luca took them to. He, Ty, and Colin came back an hour ago. After they filled everyone in on what they learned about the radioactive material, they decided they needed to visit Luca's mother to see what she could tell them. Clary wasn't going to argue. She wanted answers.

The front door opened and a slender woman with dark hair and eyes to match her son's stood in the entryway. She smiled as she caught sight of them, then stepped forward to give Luca a peck on the cheek.

"Come in, please." She stood to the side and ushered them all in, shutting the door behind them. "Let's go sit in the family room." She led them down a hallway to the back of the house, where it opened up into a large room that encompassed the kitchen, dining room, and family room.

Luca grabbed a couple of chairs and brought them over to the area around the couch, then sat in one, his mom in the other. Clary and Colin perched in armchairs while Ty, Penny, and Keira sat on the couch. Leo sat on the arm next to his wife. Once they were seated, Luca introduced them all.

"So, fill me in. Luca didn't say much on the phone other than it involved Penny." Luca's mother, Meredith, glanced at Penny with a curious frown. "I tried getting a read on you, but everything was very jumbled. I think some direction could help."

Luca handed her the case he held. She sucked in a sharp breath the moment her hands touched it.

"So much destruction. Death." A frown creased her brow. "But it doesn't have to be that way. There is a path to peace."

"How?" Leo asked.

She shook her head. "I can't tell. It's just a feeling. You're involved, so nothing is crystal clear."

"What if you focus on each one of us individually?" Colin said. "On our role alone. Maybe we could piece together what's going to happen from that."

She shrugged. "It's worth a try. Who wants to go first?"

"I'm game," Ty said.

Meredith grinned. "I knew I would like you the moment I sensed you in Penny's life. That hasn't changed." She glanced at her son. "Move."

A corner of Luca's mouth quirked. "Yes, ma'am." He stood, and Ty settled into his vacated chair.

"Give me your hands," Meredith said, turning to face Ty.

He laid his hands in hers, and she closed her eyes. "Pain. I sense great pain."

"Great," Ty muttered.

"Of loss. A past loss. Your father."

"My dad died recently."

Her head bobbed once. "Yes."

"Mom, we need future stuff, not the past."

She opened her eyes to pin her son with a glare. "I'm getting there. You know this is a process."

Luca held up his hands. "Sorry."

Her lips twitched, and she closed her eyes again, suppressing her smile. She rolled her shoulders and concentrated once more. "I see you in an industrial facility. Flashing lights. Sirens." She frowned. "Tight spaces." Her eyes opened. "That's it. I'm sorry."

Ty shook his head. "Don't be. I think I know where you saw me. It validates what we've learned."

Meredith smiled. "Good." She looked over the group. "Who's next?"

They took turns sitting in the chair. Much of what she saw echoed her vision of Ty, so when it was Clary's turn, she was surprised when Meredith gasped and clutched her hands.

"What?" Clary stared at the woman, trying to see into her mind.

"Clary, you have no idea how powerful you are, do you?"

"What? What do you mean?"

"Your dreams. They're so much more. I see a journey for you. To find what was lost. But you're asleep."

A deep frown cut through Clary's face. What was she talking about? "How do I find something while I'm dreaming? And what did I lose?"

Meredith opened her eyes. "You didn't lose anything. Someone is lost. You're supposed to help them."

Help me.

Clary gasped. "No." She looked away, her mind racing. No, this couldn't be right. "Can you—see—this person?"

"Hmm." She tipped her head, a furrow forming between her eyes. "It's a woman. I can't see her face. I'm getting darkness. And light." She opened her eyes. "I'm sorry. I wish I could be more descriptive, but that's all I see."

"That's okay. It makes sense."

"It does?"

"Yes. I've been dreaming about a woman. She keeps asking me to help her, and—" Clary took a deep breath and glanced at the others. "And her skin—one half of her body is the inkiest black I've ever seen. The other is pure white. Darkness and light."

"Wait." Ty sat forward. "Black and white? With amber eyes?"

Clary's eyes widened. "How did you know?"

"Because I know who you're dreaming about." He scrubbed a hand over his face. "Damn. I don't know what to make of this."

"Make of what?" Penny asked. "Who's she dreaming about?"

He looked at her. "After dad died, I started reading some of his mythology texts. I figured someone needed to bone up on all this stuff, so we at least had a place to start if we ever needed to look something up. After Hades visited, I did some more digging. She's dreaming about Melinoe."

"No." Clary said. No, that couldn't be right. How could she be communicating with the lost goddess?

"Are you sure?" Leo asked.

Ty nodded. "It matches her description from the books." He turned to Clary. "Where are you when you talk to her?"

"Um." Clary cleared her throat and continued. "The first time, I woke up in a field, and I remember thinking it looked strange. Then, the next thing I knew, I was in some creepy forest and she was there asking me to help her. The next time, we were in the field, and she looked at a castle in the distance and asked me to help her again. It was the same the third time, except she pointed to the castle. She disappeared before I could help her get there."

"Castle?" Leo's voice was low and deadly. "Was it all black with a bunch of spiky turrets?"

Clary frowned, but nodded.

"Shit." Leo and Ty shared a look.

"What? Do you know where that is?"

"We do," Leo said. "But the question we need to answer is how you got there."

"And came back," Ty added.

Her eyes bounced between the two. "What do you mean? Where is it?"

"That's Hades's castle," Penny said, her voice soft.

"It sounds like you were in Elysium or the Asphodel Fields," Keira added. "Did you see anyone else?"

Clary's mind raced. She stared at them all blankly as she tried to process what they just said. She'd been in the underworld?

"Clary." Colin's hand landed on hers as he crouched in front of her. "This is important. Did you see anyone else? Did Melinoe give you any indication how her soul separated from her body? Or why she needed help?"

His low voice drew her out of her stupor. She looked down into his aqua-colored eyes. "There were others roaming around, but no one I recognized. They didn't seem to know we were there. And no, she only pointed to the castle. All she ever said was help me. Oh, and she knew my name. She said, 'You must help me, Clary Moncrief.'"

"Dammit." Leo pushed to his feet and paced to the window. "This isn't good. If Hades finds out she can communicate with his daughter, he might try to take her to the underworld to help him search for her."

"He'll what?" Clary looked over at him, alarmed. "I'm not going anywhere with him."

"Trust me, he won't give you a choice," Leo growled.

Clary swallowed hard. "I don't understand any of this. I mean, it was just a dream. I have lucid dreams all the time."

"But it wasn't a dream," Meredith said. "Yes, technically, you were asleep, but your mind traveled to another plane."

"How?"

Meredith shrugged. "Thank your heritage. Like I said, you're much more powerful than you know. In my vision, I saw you linked to another mind. Colin's." She pointed at him. "The two of you were in a forest together."

"A forest?" Colin said. "Could it be the one she saw Melinoe in?"

"It's possible."

"But why would I be with her?"

"I don't know. You just were."

"Hang on a second." Clary held up a hand. "I can link my mind to others?"

Meredith nodded. "Yes. It's one of your gifts. Through dreams, you're able to link your mind to another person's. Your mind pulls them in. It's a form of telepathy."

Clary's eyes met Colin's. Heat licked up her neck to redden her cheeks as the memory of her dream about him the other night resurfaced. Recognition dawned in his eyes, and she knew it hadn't been just a dream.

Colin cleared his throat and looked at Meredith. "So, how does this help us?"

"I'm not sure, but I think if you want to find Melinoe's soul, Clary's the key."

"Okay, I get that Melinoe was Phobos and Deimos's first victim in this war, but how does finding her help us?" Keira asked.

"It probably doesn't," Leo said. "But finding her helps restore the balance. I think we have to if we want any peace from Hades."

Ty waved a hand. "Let's put that on the back burner. We need to focus on stopping Phobos and Deimos first. Mrs. Vasco, is there anything you can tell us to help us find them?"

"Not that I saw—"

"Wait," Clary said. She scooted forward in her chair. As they talked, her mind had whirled through the information she just learned and sparked an idea. "What if I tried to link to Brandon?"

"No. Absolutely not," Colin said.

"Hear me out. I would control the whole thing, because it's a construct of my mind. I might be able to get him to reveal where he is without him even knowing what's happening."

"No. It's too dangerous." Colin's jaw worked. "What if he hypnotizes you while you're together?"

"At the first hint of him trying that, I'll end the dream."

"So you say. What if you recognize it too late?"

"It'll only be too late if I don't. And I'll know long before he can get me to that point. There's a certain speech pattern that needs to be used for hypnosis."

"I still don't like it. What if you accidentally link to Phobos and Deimos like you did—" he broke off. His cheeks reddened, and he looked away.

Clary felt her own face flame again, but did her best to ignore it. She didn't want to broadcast to everyone what happened. "I won't. Not now that I know what's going on. The knowledge will help me control the dream to a higher degree."

Colin sighed. "I'm not going to win this argument, am I?"

She shook her head.

"Fine. Just—be careful?"

"Of course." They shared a long look.

"Mom, is there anything else you can tell us?" Luca broke the silence.

Meredith sighed. "From what I've pieced together looking at all of your futures, the road ahead is rough. Tragedy will strike, but where and how that happens, I don't know. Just be prepared."

"We will."

Clary hoped he wasn't fooling himself. She didn't know how they could ever be fully prepared for what was coming.

CHAPTER 21

C louds scuttled across the moon, carried by the swift breeze. Clary stared out the window at the darkened grounds, her mind a tangle of thoughts. She should be sleeping, but nothing she tried shut her mind off. There was just too much new information to process.

After they returned from the Vasco's, Clary did some digging on Morpheus and explored her mind, trying to figure out what she could do. She should have done it the day she discovered what and who she was, but truthfully, she'd been in denial. She still wanted to be, but couldn't.

A knock sounded on her door, and she turned to look at it, then at the clock. The glowing red numbers told her it was much too late for anyone to pay her a social call.

"Clary?" Colin's voice carried through the door. "Are you awake?"

Her body tightened as her mind replayed their shared dream. If she opened the door, would things play out the same way? Would their conscious minds let them? She didn't know. But she did know she would be okay with that. The man stirred her body—and mind—in ways no man ever had.

It was that thought that carried her feet across the room to open the door.

"Couldn't sleep either?" she asked. Clary kept her eyes glued to his. If she looked lower at his sculpted chest outlined by his tight olive-green t-shirt, or even further south at his sweat pant covered lower half, she'd lose all higher functions.

He shook his head. "My brain won't shut off. Plus, I think we need to talk."

Clary nodded and stepped back so he could come in. She walked to the bed and sat down on the edge, folding her hands in her lap. He followed her, and after a brief hesitation, sat down beside her. The bed dipped, and she shot a hand out to stop from falling into him. Before she could pull it back, he covered it with his own.

"You know," he picked up her hand and stared at it, shifting his fingers to thread them through hers as he spoke, "I've never been a relationship kind of man. My life has been one fraught with danger. Special Forces doesn't leave much room for healthy relationships. Once I left the military, it had been so long since I even thought about having more than a few dates with a woman that I forgot what a relationship felt like." His eyes caught hers. "I want that with you. I don't want a quick roll in bed, then to say goodbye once we catch Henley and stop Phobos and Deimos. That dream—" He looked away and took a breath. "I know it was all in our minds, but it certainly felt real. The connection—I didn't imagine that, did I?"

She shook her head, swallowing to wet her suddenly dry mouth. "No. No, that part was real. Is real. But is now the right time for us to make a decision like this? Doesn't intense pressure—danger—make us make rash decisions?"

He shrugged. "Maybe. But it doesn't change the fact that you make me want what I haven't wanted since I was a kid."

Clary stared at their clasped hands. She wanted more than a good time in bed too. But she'd known this man less than a week. Her brain was so chaotic right now, she didn't know what to make of their connection. Her body screamed for her to say yes to a relationship, but this was about more than what made her feel good. It was about her future.

She looked up into his aqua eyes, searching for an answer. But that could only come from within. Could she trust he would make her happy long-term? That he wouldn't turn into some alpha jackass who kept her satisfied in bed, but nowhere else? She'd dated her fair share of those.

As she considered that, she couldn't help but think of how he'd treated her so far. Colin personified courteous southern gentleman. Not once did she see an asshole side come out.

His thumb, which had been stroking the outside of hers, suddenly flicked higher, hitting the pulse point on her wrist. Clary's heart skipped a beat. None of the jerks she dated—even the ones that made her scream their names—could do that to her with such an innocent touch.

Plus, when would she ever find another man who shared her heritage or had knowledge of it?

Instead of answering, she leaned in and pressed a soft kiss to his lips. He kissed her back for a moment, then pulled away.

"Just to clarify, what are we doing? I don't want to read this wrong."

Clary smiled. "For tonight, I just want to sleep. But I want what you want. To give us a chance. I've never met a man like you."

He returned her smile and gave her a tender but intense kiss, which curled her toes.

"Sleep, huh?" He rested his forehead against hers.

She nodded. "Yeah."

"Okay." He stood and grabbed the top of the blanket. "I hope you don't snore. That's a deal breaker."

Clary laughed. "Same, buddy."

Colin smiled and held the covers up so she could climb in, then settled them around her before turning off the light and climbing in beside her. Her heart skipped as he tucked in close behind her. Arousal surged, but she stayed put. Despite what their minds thought in the dream universe, she wasn't ready to give all of herself to him just yet. She wanted rest and a clear head before that happened.

"So, do you think your mind will find mine while we sleep?" His deep voice rumbled low in her ear, and Clary shivered.

"Maybe. I'll try to keep things PG, though."

He hummed. "I'm okay with x-rated."

His thumb brushed the underside of her breast, and she bit back a moan. "Behave. It's late, and we both should go into anything further with a clear head."

Colin brushed her hair away from her neck and buried his nose there, taking a deep breath before placing a soft kiss behind her ear. "You're right. Doesn't mean I like it, but I understand. Even agree." He kissed the back of her head. "Goodnight, Clary."

"Goodnight," she whispered. Clary squeezed her eyes shut and tried not to think about him right behind her. Considering he had an arm wrapped around her waist and she could feel the solid length of his body at her back, it was difficult. But the longer she laid there, the drowsier she became until she felt her mind drift and she fell asleep.

CHAPTER 22

"What the hell?" Colin turned a full circle, staring up at the strange sky above him. Tall grass waved in a warm breeze. In the distance, he could see water shimmering in the sun—from a sun he couldn't see.

"Seriously? We have to stop meeting like this."

Colin turned to see Clary walking toward him. "What's going on? Where are we? I thought you weren't going to pull me into your dreams again."

She shrugged and stopped in front of him. "I didn't do it intentionally. I just fell asleep. Then I woke up here and there you were."

"Where's here? Is this the place you were talking about earlier?" He glanced around again.

She nodded. "Yeah. Elysium." Her face scrunched. "I still don't know how I keep ending up here. I hope Hades doesn't find out. I don't want to get stuck here."

Unease skated up Colin's spine. He didn't want that either. "Come on, let's walk. Maybe we can find Melinoe and help her." He held a hand out to her.

She took it and let him lead her through the swaying grass. They walked for several minutes, the sound of the grass blowing in the wind the only sound. A few souls passed them, their peace washing over them as they walked by. Colin felt himself relax the longer they walked. His mind knew they were in the afterlife, but he didn't think it was so bad. At least, not here. He was sure what laid past the black clouds to their left was beyond his wildest nightmares.

"Colin?"

A new voice intruded on their walk. One he recognized, but hadn't heard in months. Colin's spine stiffened and his shoulders went taut. Slowly, he turned, his eyes widening as he saw the giant of a man who said his name. "Jack?"

"Oh my God. Son, what are you doing here? How did you get here? And who's this?"

"Colin?" Clary looked up at him, confusion on her pretty face.

Colin swallowed hard, scarcely believing his eyes. He squeezed them shut. "No. This is just a dream. You aren't real." He was *not* talking to his partner's dead father. But when he opened his eyes, Jack Farris was still there.

"Colin," Jack laid a hand on his arm. Tingles raced through Colin's body at the touch. It was like touching pure peace and love. "Are you—did you—" He broke off.

"I'm not dead, no," he reassured him. "And Ty's fine too."

Relief relaxed Jack's shoulders. "That's good to hear. But it doesn't explain why you're here or how you got here." He leaned forward, lowering his voice. "This is Elysium. The afterlife. It's not a realm for living souls."

"I know. And we're not sure how we got here or why we're here. Jack, this is Clary Moncrief. Long story short, Hecate had a backup plan. She convinced Ares's sons, Phobos and Deimos, to spread fear and dread among humans to start a war, and they enlisted a hypnotist with divine ancestry to help them do it. Clary is his colleague. She can control her dreams and those of others, which is why I'm here. She pulled me in somehow."

Jack frowned. "What does all that have to do with why you're in the underworld?"

"We think it has something to do with Melinoe," Clary said. "Phobos and Deimos split her from herself. They put into some kind of stasis, almost like death, then sent her soul somewhere she can't get back from. I think she's calling me here to help her," Clary said. "She keeps showing up and saying, 'help me.' Except, I don't know how. She just points at Hades's castle and says help."

Jack rubbed his jaw and stared past them. "Oh my. Hades and Persephone must be quite distraught."

Colin snorted. "Enough so that they showed up at Ty and Penny's, asking for help because the Oracle told them to."

Jack's eyes widened. "The Oracle sent them to you?"

They nodded.

"Oh my."

"Why do you keep saying that?" Colin asked. "Does what the Oracle said mean something bad?"

"Not necessarily. It just means that the line between worlds is blurring. The boundary weakening."

"How is that not a bad thing?"

"It is, but it may not be permanent. And in the end, what you and the others do could strengthen it."

"How?"

"By finding Melinoe and restoring her soul."

"I'm confused," Clary said. "How does Melinoe's soul and my colleague's plan to hypnotize all of humanity relate to each other?"

"Melinoe is a conduit. She helps lost souls reach the afterlife. Without her, many will wander Earth for eternity, their energies coming into contact with one another and the living as well, feeding off each other until the line between life and death becomes—blurred. There will still be absolutes, but you'll see more people claiming mental illness, saying they see ghosts. If your friend has divine ancestry, he will likely be able to hypnotize spirits. Phobos and Deimos can help them cross, then they'll wreak havoc here, upsetting the balance in the underworld. Perhaps even overthrowing Hades."

Colin snapped his fingers to point at Clary. "That's their plan. If they're all dead, they all come here." He looked at Jack. "Would Melinoe let a hypnotized soul into the underworld?"

Jack shook his head. "No. She would want them to make the choice of where they want to be for themselves. A hypnotized soul can't do that."

"We need to find her," Colin said. "Help her get where she needs to go and stop this. Do you know where she might be?"

Jack shook his head. "No, but I'll do some digging. Hades was kind enough to make sure I ended up in Elysium. There are some powerful old gods here. I'll talk to them."

Colin let out a short chuckle. "I never thought I'd hear the word kind associated with Hades. He's an ass."

Jack smiled. "He is, but he has a heart. Weird, I know." He made a shooing motion with his hands. "You two should get out of here. Let me gather some information and come back tomorrow."

Clary snorted. "If we can. I don't have a clue how I keep ending up here."

"Melinoe's out there somewhere. She has a hand in it, I think. You'll be back, I'm sure of it." His face sobered. "I just wish you could bring my son. I know his mother would love to see him. And his sister."

Colin felt tears prick his eyes, happy that Jack was reunited with his family. "They're here?"

Jack nodded. "They stayed back when I saw you. Souls are wary of outsiders. There's an order down here that rarely gets upset."

He cleared his throat. "Well, tell them I'm happy you're all together again."

"I will."

Colin's vision grew dark. "Clary?"

"We're losing the dream," she said.

He turned back to Jack.

"Tell Ty I said I love him. Penny too." Jack reached a hand out, skimming Colin's arm with his fingers, then he faded away. Blackness engulfed Colin's vision, and he sank into a deep sleep.

CHAPTER 23

C lary stirred as the bed moved. She opened her eyes to see Colin sitting up next to her. He looked down, eyes wide.

"Did that really happen?"

She sat up. "Yeah. And now we know their endgame."

He flipped back the covers and stood. "We need to wake the others."

"Can I get dressed first?" She swung her legs over the bed.

Colin looked back. His eyes darkened as he took in her skimpy pajamas. He cleared his throat. "That would probably be a good idea."

A corner of her mouth lifted as she noted his response to her limited attire. "Make sure you put on jeans. Someone wants to play."

His face reddened, and he looked down at his waist. "Yeah, well, he wants to experience your perfect body for himself."

Clary's body clenched, and desire flooded her veins. Well-rested and in the light of day, she wanted this man more than she did last night. Reservations gone now that she'd slept on it. She licked her lips. "Maybe we should let him."

Colin's shoulders straightened. He stalked around the bed to stand in front of her. "It is early still. We could let everyone sleep for a while yet."

She nodded and stood, snaking her arms up around his neck and gripping the hair on the back of his head. "Yeah."

His hands cupped her butt and pulled her into him. His erection pressed against her belly. Clary's eyes fluttered as arousal threatened to overwhelm her.

"Do you have protection in here?"

She opened her eyes to look at him. "No. But I'm on the pill."

"Good enough for me." He ducked his head and took her mouth in a searing kiss.

Clary kissed him back with her entire being. She fought the urge to climb him like a tree. His mouth left hers to trail down her neck.

"Should we recreate what our minds did?" He nuzzled the hollow at the top of her satin tank.

Need left her mind fuzzy, and it took her a moment to register what he said. She swallowed to wet her parched mouth—all the moisture in her body had fled south. "I don't care what we do, so long as we end up naked with you inside me."

"That can be arranged." He pulled back, whisking her top over her head. He kissed her again, palming her breasts as his tongue plundered her mouth.

She clutched his arms, holding herself up as pulses of pure need shot through her with every tweak of her nipple between his fingers. Wanting to feel his chest against hers, she sought the bottom of his shirt, her nails raking his skin as she rucked up the fabric. He groaned and pulled away to whip it over his head.

Clary ran a hand over the ink on his ribcage. "I love your tattoos. They tell a great story."

"They're a reminder. To never take life for granted. It's too short."

She agreed. Which was why she was standing here half-naked in his arms after having only known him for five days. Standing on her toes, she sealed her mouth to his.

It was the catalyst they needed to take things to the next level. Gone were the exploratory, cautious touches. Their hands roamed each other's bodies with surety, remembering what gave the other pleasure. They rid themselves of their remaining clothes, then toppled onto the bed. Clary tried to wrap her legs around him and draw him into her, but he lifted his hips and came to rest beside her.

"Not yet. I'm going to take my time." He leaned down and ran his tongue over her breast, drawing the tip into his mouth. Plucking at the other one with his fingers, he drew her into a frenzy. Clary had never come before with a man just touching her breasts, but she was dangerously close now.

She knew he knew, too. He smiled against her skin, then ran a hand down her body, skimming the sides of her mound. Her hips bucked, and she moaned.

"I see your mind had this part right. Your body is very responsive."

"Only to you," she breathed. "It just wants you."

He grinned. "Let's see how true that is." He pushed up on his hands and swung his hips over hers, teasing her with his erection while suckling her breasts.

Pleasure rocketed through Clary as her first orgasm hit, sending her soaring into the clouds. She rolled her hips against him, still wanting more. "More."

"As you wish." He flipped her over and pushed her legs apart, squeezing the globes of her butt in his hands.

Clary moaned. If he didn't touch her where she wanted most soon, she would be forced to take matters into her own hands.

He gripped her hips and lifted her until she was on her knees. She let out a squeak of surprise as he nipped at her rear. Heat flooded her core and moisture pooled.

He gave a low chuckle. "Sorry, couldn't resist."

"That's okay. Do it again."

"Mmm. I have a better idea."

Before she could ask what that was, his tongue swiped through her wet folds. Clary moaned, loud and long. She felt him smile against her, then he probed her entrance. He brought a hand up to swirl around that little nub of nerves. Her breath escaped in a quick puff, then her body spasmed around the finger he slid into her channel. She buried her face in the pillow to muffle her shout as her second climax in as many minutes sent her flying.

A shout that turned into another loud moan as his thick, hard shaft replaced his finger. Dear God, he felt good. Feeling full to the point of pain, she blew out a breath and let her muscles relax to accommodate his girth. He held himself still, except for that damn hand of his, which continued to swirl through her folds.

"Are you good?" he growled in her ear.

She nodded. "Yes. I need you to move. Now." The last word came out as a breathy whisper.

He flexed his hips, sending shock waves through Clary.

"Like that?"

"Yes," she hissed. She pushed back to meet his thrust.

He gripped her hips and pounded into her. Clary braced her hands against the headboard and held on as he took her for a ride. She was glad he'd already given her two orgasms. It meant she could hold out longer and take him over the mountain with her. When his pace faltered, she knew he was close, so she clenched her inner muscles, increasing the friction for them both. One stroke and she broke. She let go of the headboard and put her face in the pillows to muffle her scream.

Colin didn't have that luxury. His harsh shout filled the room before he cut it off with a low groan.

Clary's legs gave out, and she slid into a boneless heap on her belly. He followed her down and moved to the side to keep from crushing her.

"That was better than the dream," she mumbled.

He chuckled. "Definitely."

She sighed. "I suppose we should get up, though. Saving the world and all that."

"Yeah." He rolled to his back.

Clary turned her head to look at him.

"I wish we could stay here. I've never run from a fight in my life, but this is one I wish we didn't have to fight."

She traced the words on his ribcage. "Me too. But if we don't, where does that leave us?"

"Unable to have a life together."

"Exactly." She rolled onto her side and sat up. "And I don't know about you, but I want more of this—" she wagged a finger between them, "for longer than just the next few days."

A wicked grin split his handsome face, ratcheting Clary's pulse higher. God, he was gorgeous.

"Then that's what we fight for. More sex."

She laughed. "Forget saving the world. We're doing it for sex."

He leaned over and kissed her. "Come on. Let's wash up, then go find the others. We need to make a plan to find Henley."

Clary sighed and got up. She reached for her clothes, but Colin standing in front of her stopped her. She glanced at him. A grin slashed his face.

"I think a shower's in order, don't you?"

She echoed his smile. "I like the way you think."

He pulled her into him and lifted her off her feet, then walked toward the bathroom.

CHAPTER 24

"Wait a second." Ty frowned at Clary as they all sat around the living room an hour later. "You've been dreaming about the underworld? And you saw my dad? Like, for real?"

"Yes. I know it sounds crazy, but it's true." She wished she knew how it was possible. It shouldn't be. Especially the underworld part. That freaked her out.

He turned to Colin. "And you were there?"

Colin nodded.

"Why you and not me? He's my father."

"Clary and I have some kind of—connection. She's been pulling me into her dreams, but we don't know how or why."

"I think all of that is irrelevant right now," Leo said. "We need to focus on what they learned, that the goal is to get all those souls into the underworld and overwhelm Hades. How do we stop them?"

"We need to find Henley before he can broadcast a hypnosis session," Luca said. "I've put out some feelers, but nothing's come back. I think our best bet might be Savannah River, though. For what they want to do—they're going to need a lot of fissile material. If that much was missing from that site, we'd have heard about it. My guess is they're planning something. Something that will let them get away with a lot of nuclear waste."

"Maybe," Leo said. "But think about it. He can hypnotize people to do things against their will. How do we know he didn't get the staff to cover up the theft? We know they have material from there. Maybe they stole it all at once."

"So, how do we determine if it's missing already?" Clary asked.

"Short of tipping our hand to the non-divine authorities, I don't think we do," Ty said. He sighed and pinched the bridge of his nose. "We need to operate under the assumption they already have it."

"Okay, so where does that leave us?" Penny asked.

"Figuring out where they're going to strike," Leo said. "If I were Henley, and I wanted to hypnotize as many people as possible all at once, what's the best way to do that?"

"Through the media," Keira said. "TV, radio, social media sites."

"Exactly. And New Year's Eve is in two days. People all around the world will be glued to TV screens, watching the celebrations. If I were him, I'd broadcast myself worldwide that night."

"Okay," Luca said. "So, we're looking for a place he can broadcast. He'd need a fairly sophisticated setup for that, wouldn't he?"

"Not necessarily," Leo said. "With today's technology, he'd just need a few high-end laptops, a camera, internet service, and someone who knows what they're doing."

"I know someone who can help," Colin said. "My hacker friend, Charisse. She might be able to get us a location. A lot of those types know each other. Or know of each other. I could ask her to check some of their chatrooms and see if she can dig up anything."

Leo nodded. "Do it. Clary, tonight, you need to try to pull Henley into a dream. Take Colin with you if you want."

"I want," Colin said.

Clary looked at him and nodded. She wasn't keen on confronting Brandon alone. Not because she was afraid of him, but because she didn't know what all to ask.

"Although, *chère*, do you think it would be possible to put a locator spell on him in the dream?" Leo looked at his wife.

Keira frowned, then shook her head. "I don't think so. He'd need to ingest a potion. If I had something from him—blood, hair—he wouldn't need to drink anything for me to get a read. I'd just need a map."

"Wait. What about his house or his boat? There has to be some of that there," Colin said.

Leo nodded. "Good point. Hang tight." He vanished, the front door slamming as he left.

Keira sighed and put a hand over her belly. "I'm really hoping this child doesn't inherit his speed. I'll never be able to keep up."

Penny laughed. "Especially if it gets your mouth and his smarts."

A wave of pure joy washed over Clary, reminding her of the rainbow in the void. She cocked her head and looked at Keira.

"Keira, do you ever dream about your baby?"

She frowned. "Of course."

"What do you see?"

"Nothing concrete. The vague outline of a child running. Laughing. Lots of sunshine and happiness. Why?"

Clary bit her lip and rose from her chair, walking over to crouch in front of Keira. She held out a hand near her mid-section. "May I?"

Keira glanced down, then at Clary. "What's going on?"

"Your baby's sleeping right now, isn't it?"

"I think so, yes." Her frown deepened. "How do you know that?"

"Because I'm sensing its dream. And I think I've been tapping into it the last couple of nights."

"What?" Keira's eyes grew large. "What's it look like?"

"Rainbows. And happiness." She pointed to Keira's abdomen again. "May I?"

After a moment, Keira nodded. Clary laid her hand over Keira's stomach and closed her eyes. The same image she saw in her dreams entered her mind. Colors swirled behind her eyes and joy filled her heart. And this time, there was a new emotion. Love.

Clary smiled, keeping her eyes closed. She held out her free hand. "Give me your hand."

Keira's fingers closed around hers.

"Now close your eyes." Clary waited a beat, then let the images flow through her to Keira.

"Oh my God! Is that—?"

"Your baby, yes. He or she loves you very much. They're dreaming about you." Even at such an early stage, the bond between mother and child was strong. It amazed Clary the depth of emotion present. The images faded, and she opened her eyes, smiling at Keira.

Tears ran down Keira's cheeks. "That was incredible."

A breeze hit them at the same moment Leo appeared. The triumphant smile on his face died as he took in the tears on Keira's face.

"What happened? Why are you crying?" His brown eyes turned hard, and he glared at Clary. "What did you do?"

Colin stepped between them. "Back off. She would never hurt her, you know that."

Leo blew out a breath. "You're right. Sorry. I'm just a little overprotective at the moment."

Clary stood up and smiled at him. "No worries. I understand."

Keira rose to stand next to her. "She was showing me our baby's dream. It was beautiful."

His mouth went slack. "What? And I missed it?"

"I'd show you, but the dream stopped," Clary said. "Next time."

He nodded, studying her. "I'm sorry, again. To be honest, your abilities freak me out a bit. Hades got in my head when he stole my soul. So did Athena when she unleashed my powers. It wasn't a comfortable feeling."

"I understand. Trust me, it's not something I'm that comfortable with, either. I'm still learning to control it. And sometimes, it just hits me, like it did with the baby." She glanced away.

"So, did you find anything on your little jaunt?" Colin asked.

"Yes." Leo held up a small plastic bag with a few strands of hair inside. "I found these on his bed."

Keira snatched the bag from his hands. "I'm taking full advantage of the baby's nap. Let's go find us a baddie." She turned and left the room, headed for the stairs.

Clary looked at Colin, who shrugged. He took her hand, and they followed her, along with the others, to the magic room. Keira stopped behind the desk and grabbed a few items from the shelves on the wall. They looked on as she added ingredients to a clean jar, then added water and swirled it around. With a pair of tweezers, she took the hair from the bag and added it to the liquid, swirling it again.

Without a word, she held her hand out to her husband. He pulled a signet ring off his finger and gave it to her. She looped a leather cord through it, then dunked it in the mixture in the jar.

"Which map do you want, *chère*?"

"Oh, let's start with South Carolina. Maybe we'll get lucky."

Leo rummaged through the desk drawer and withdrew a map, unfolding it over the desk's surface. Keira took the ring from the jar and let it drip, then held it over the map, muttering something to herself. Clary watched as the ring pulled against the cord and pointed toward a corner of the map.

"Whoa," Colin said.

"That's freaky." Clary stared at the ring, trying to process its gravity-defying orientation.

"That's the power of the world around us, telling us where to go." Keira moved the ring in the direction it pointed. "With a little help." She got to the edge, but it still pointed away from her. "I need the southern U.S. map."

Leo opened the drawer again and found the map she wanted, spreading it over the state map. The ring surged toward Georgia. Keira followed it until it hung over an area just outside of Augusta.

Luca leaned in and pointed to a place on the map. "That's the Savannah River site."

"That makes sense," Ty said. "If they're planning on detonating bombs, nuclear sites would be a good way to spread radioactive material without the need for a dirty bomb."

"But why would he stay that close?" Clary couldn't see Brandon offering himself up as a martyr. He was too narcissistic.

"He's got two gods working with him. Maybe he thinks they'll shield him from the blast somehow." Ty shrugged.

She tipped her head in acknowledgement. He was just arrogant enough to think that. "Okay. So, what's the plan now?" She looked at Leo.

"We go to Savannah River. And you find Melinoe's soul. If we fail to stop them, we're going to need her to keep all those souls out of the underworld."

"No pressure." Clary folded her arms, her mouth a grim line. Tonight, it sounded like she was going on a walk through the underworld.

CHAPTER 25

"**A**re you sure you're up for this?" Colin caressed Clary's bare hip under the covers, his voice quiet in the dark room.

She rolled to look at him in the low light, running her thumb over his cheekbone and sifting her fingers into his hair on the side of his head. She loved that he was concerned about her. "Yeah. I'll have you there. And Ty, if I can manage to pull him in with us. My only worry is we won't find her. And we really only have tonight. I'm just glad Keira could come up with something to not only sync our sleep cycles but to extend our REM sleep and to help us pick up where we were when we leave it."

"Our bodies are going to hate us for it in the morning, though."

"One night won't hurt much. I think it's necessary for what we want to accomplish."

"I agree." He leaned in and gave her a gentle kiss. "Should we put clothes on first?" he asked when he pulled back.

Clary laughed, then rubbed against him, enjoying the feel of his nakedness against hers. "No. We've been dressed in regular clothes so far. Well, except for the sex dream, but that was different."

He nuzzled her neck. "Good. I like sleeping naked next to you."

Clary practically purred. "Same, detective. Same." One large hand landed on her butt to hold her steady while he ground against her. She gasped, but smacked his chest. "Behave. You already got to play."

"I know. But I've gotten a second wind."

She bit back a moan and smacked his chest again, then nudged him away. "We have work to do."

He sighed and let her go, rolling to his back and tucking her into his side. "Fine. Can we have a sex dream first, though?"

She let loose a full-blown laugh. Nestling into the crook of his arm, she laid a hand over his diaphragm. "We'll see. I don't know what my mind will do."

He hummed. "So long as Ty's not involved in that. I don't share."

"Me either." She reached up and pecked a kiss onto his chin. "Goodnight."

"Goodnight." He dropped a kiss on top of her head and sank into the pillows.

Clary closed her eyes and did her best to shove out the thoughts of the naked man in her arms and what she wanted to do to him, so she could sleep.

CHAPTER 26

"I really hoped to never see this place again. At least not until I died." Ty looked around, a deep frown on his face.

Colin patted him on the back. "Sorry. But there's a bonus." He nodded to the right.

Clary turned, as did Ty, and saw Jack walking toward them, two women in tow.

Ty straightened to his full height. "Mom?" His voice broke.

A smile wreathed the older woman's face. She hurried forward with her arms out. In two long strides, Ty was in her arms.

"How long has it been since they've seen each other?" Clary asked Colin.

"He was only three or four when she died in childbirth."

"Who's the other woman?" Clary eyed the tall, dark-haired woman up and down. She looked familiar.

"I'm not sure."

Ty pulled back to look in his mother's face. "This hardly seems real." He turned his attention to Jack. "Dad."

A grin split Jack's face. "Son." He held his arms open. Ty stepped away from his mom to give Jack a hug. "It's good to see you, Ty." He let go to look into Ty's face. "How's your wife?"

"She's good. We all are." Ty sniffed and stepped back. He glanced at the young woman at his mom's side. "Who's this?"

The woman smiled. "I'm your sister. Diana."

"What?" Ty's eyes were wide. Clary knew hers were too. "How is that possible? You were a baby."

"There are no children in Heaven and Hell," Jack said. "Only our mature souls."

"Well," Ty cleared his throat, "it's nice to meet you." He held out a hand.

She took it, then pulled him close for a hug. "You too. Mom and Dad have told me a lot about you."

"We've spent a lot of time getting acquainted in the last few months." Jack smiled at both his children. "But a lengthy reunion will have to wait. You three are on a time crunch."

"We are." Colin stepped forward, speaking for Ty and giving him a chance to compose himself. "Did you learn anything?"

"I did. Beyond the clouds in Tartarus, there's a place where souls roam, lost. They're doomed to wander for eternity."

"So, how do we get her out?" Ty asked.

"She must be bound to her body again and brought out."

Ty groaned. "Great. That means we need to talk to Hades. He and Persephone have Melinoe's body."

"I don't think they'll have a problem turning her over to you. They may even want to help. But you should go now. You haven't much time. The first hypnotized souls have already crossed. And I'm sure more are piling up among the living."

Colin gave a curt nod. "Okay. Thank you for your help, Jack."

Ty hugged his family again. Clary turned to look at the castle. They'd never make it there and then into Tartarus tonight without help.

"How do we do this?" She looked at Colin and motioned to the castle in the distance.

"This is a dream, remember? You control it. Take us there."

She resisted the urge to smack her forehead. It was difficult to remember this was a dream. The whole thing felt so real. "Right." She glanced at Ty. "Are you ready?"

He gave his mother's hand a last squeeze, then turned to her and nodded. "Let's do this."

Clary took their hands and closed her eyes. When she opened them, they were standing in front of the gigantic black-lacquered doors of the palace.

Ty blew out a breath and banged his fist on the door. Clary couldn't stop the laugh that burst free.

He glanced at her and cocked an eyebrow. "Why are you laughing?"

"We're *knocking* on Hades's front door." She shrugged. "Like we would at any other person's house. It just feels like there should be some sort of loud, over-the-top doorbell." She laughed again. "You used your fist on a twenty-foot door."

A smile quirked his mouth, but it quickly died as the doors swung open to reveal one of Hades's demons. Its black skin stretched tight over sinewy muscles. Horns curled from its head and red eyes glowed in its face. Clary took an instinctive step toward Colin.

"We need to talk to Hades. And Persephone, if she's around." Ty's voice brooked no argument. The demon studied him for a moment, then seemed to decide it wasn't his call what happened to the humans on his master's doorstep and beckoned them inside.

"Wait here," it rasped, then disappeared up the stairs.

In its absence, Clary took the chance to study her surroundings. It was not what she expected from the lord of the underworld. Oh, there was marble everywhere, but it was tasteful and light. She figured the castle would be all dark wood and shiny black marble or granite. Instead, she walked on bright white marble floors and was surrounded by white walls. The staircase unfolding in front of them was wood, though. Intricately carved with scenes like she'd only ever seen in books, the banister was a deep, rich mahogany. She glanced up, expecting to see frescoes on the ceiling, but it was a smooth white, trimmed by wide moldings.

When she looked down again, she jumped. Hades stood in front of her.

She narrowed her eyes at him. "You delight in scaring people." It really wasn't a question. Amusement lit his eyes.

He smiled. "It's part of the job description." His smile died, and he looked them over. "Now, why are you here? Better yet, how did you get here? None of you are dead."

"We're dreaming," she said.

A frown creased his eyebrows. "What?"

"Dreaming. That thing people do when they sleep?" Ty said.

"I know what dreaming is, smart-ass. But I'm not."

"No. It's a weird mix of dream and reality." Clary twisted her mouth. "I'm not sure how it works, or even how we got here." She held up a finger. "We know why we're here, though."

Hades folded his arms over his massive chest. Muscles bulged and strained his clothes. Clary tried not to think about how he could snuff out her existence with his thumb.

"We need Melinoe's body."

He dropped his arms. "What?" His voice thundered through the foyer.

"To reunite her with her soul." She held out her hands. "We think we know where she is."

"You know where my baby is?" Persephone appeared next to Hades. "How?"

Clary blinked. Ty picked up where she left off.

"My dad's here, remember? Clary came across him in another dream and talked to him. He asked around Elysium and got some information for us. He thinks she's in a place in Tartarus where lost souls wander."

Hades frowned. "I looked there."

"Maybe *you* can't find her," Colin said. "Everything else involves us. Why wouldn't this be the same?"

Persephone frowned and looked at Hades. "He has a point."

"Plus, we aren't really here," Clary said. "Maybe you can't see her because you're living. We're basically apparitions, like she is."

He ran his hands through his hair, clutching the strands, before crossing his arms again. "Fine. But you'll need some assistance. Protection." He snapped his fingers.

Some sort of lightweight metal armor appeared on all of them. Swords hung off Colin's and Ty's belts.

"Hey, why am I weaponless?" She looked down at her belt, then up at Hades, lifting an eyebrow.

Hades sighed and snapped his fingers again. A short sword appeared at her hip. "Happy?"

She smiled. "Yes, thank you. Girls can fight, too, you know."

Persephone chuckled. "I like you."

Hades rolled his eyes. "Here." He held up a hand and opened it. A glass orb sat in his palm. "You'll need this. It will allow you to transport Melinoe's soul. Then you don't have to haul her body around. Bring it back here and we'll reunite her."

Clary took the orb. "Um..." She looked at her outfit. There was no place to store it.

Sensing her conundrum, Hades snapped his fingers once more. A small pouch appeared on her belt.

"Perfect." She put the orb inside, then looked at Ty and Colin. "You two ready?"

They nodded and held their hands out to her. She took them and offered the two gods a smile, then closed her eyes.

CHAPTER 27

Unease skittered down Colin's spine as he opened his eyes. Black fog swirled around them, obscuring his vision. An orange glow permeated everything, and a faint roar of flames reached his ears. He did not want to see the fire that caused it.

"How are we supposed to find anyone in this?" Ty asked.

"Maybe she'll come to us." Clary closed her eyes. "Melinoe. We're here. Can you hear me?"

"Help me."

Clary's eyes snapped open at the whisper carried on the wind. "Did you hear that?"

"Yeah." Colin spun around, looking for the source of the voice. "I don't see anyone."

"Clary Moncrief, help me."

"Can you tell where it's coming from?" Ty asked her. "She's speaking to you."

"Maybe. That way, I think." Clary pointed to her left.

"Good enough for me. At least it's a place to start." Colin drew his sword. "Let's go."

The three of them ran into the fog.

"Anything?" Ty looked all around as they moved. He twirled his sword with a quick roll of his wrist. Tension lined his wide shoulders.

Clary shook her head, her own sword now in her hand. "No. Just keep going."

With cautious steps, they advanced, moving toward whatever drew Clary into the fog. Colin hoped it was Melinoe and not something out to trick them.

A low snarl sounded to his left. They froze.

"What was that?" Clary's voice shook. She held her sword out.

The high shriek of something wild sounded behind them, spinning them around. They moved together, their backs against each other. Another shriek sounded overhead.

"Shit. They can fly?" Ty said.

Colin looked up, but only saw more of the black fog. A shadow crossed in the corner of his eye. "There! What was that?" He pointed to the right. A wing flapped, sending the dark clouds spinning toward them.

"I don't want to know." Clary tugged on his shirttail. "Let's keep moving."

They took off running again. Clary paused several times to close her eyes and get a sense of where they needed to go. Colin kept his head on a swivel, looking for more of the winged creatures or anything else that wanted to jump out at them. As they ran, he felt a weight settle on his shoulders.

"Clary, are we falling asleep?"

She nodded. "I'm trying to keep it at bay, but I'm losing. We're going to have to pick this back up in the next dream cycle."

Blackness edged his vision. "I guess we'll find out if Keira's potion worked the way it's supposed to." The sword in his hand disappeared as sleep took hold. The world around him faded to nothingness.

CHAPTER 28

Consciousness came back to Clary with a jolt. One second, there was nothing; the next, she was on her butt inside a building in a long hallway. She peered into the gloom. Sconces flickered on the walls, the frosted glass containing their flames and providing just enough light for her to see through the darkness. Hard wood flooring covered by a plush forest green rug rested under her. Paneled walls in a deep hue stretched the length of the hall, broken only by floor-to-ceiling windows framed with gauzy curtains to let in the muted orange glow from outside.

She pushed to her feet and looked both ways. "Colin? Ty?" *Dammit.* Was she unable to pull them in with her this time? She looked down at herself. At least all her accouterments made it back. She drew the sword and shut her eyes, silently calling to Melinoe. The goddess's voice bounced around her head, closer this time.

Clary let her mind lead her to the source. She wound up an ornate staircase to the next floor, then up another. Once, she peered outside. More fog met her gaze, but she could see the building stretch beyond her and rise into a tall turret. It looked similar to the ones on Hades's palace.

Melinoe's plea led her to the turret. Clary wound her way up the spiral stone staircase to the top. It opened to a small round room. Standing at the window was Melinoe. She looked out at the ground below, but turned when Clary entered.

"Help me."

"That's why I'm here." She glanced around, making sure they were alone. "Is it really you this time?"

In a blink, Melinoe stood directly in front of her. She reached out a hand, her alabaster skin shining in the low light, and touched Clary's face. Despair, pain, grief, and fear threatened to overwhelm Clary.

She swallowed hard. "It's okay. I'm here to take you to your parents."

"I can't leave." Awareness entered Melinoe's eyes for the first time. "I'm trapped here."

Clary took the orb from the small satchel on her belt. "Your father gave me this. He and your mother are waiting for you at their palace."

Melinoe frowned. "But we're in their palace."

"We are?" She looked around. "That can't be right. We walked into the fog past the border of Tartarus."

Before the goddess could respond, a boom shook the walls.

"Time to go." Clary held up the orb. "Touch this thing so we can get out of here."

Fear paralyzed Melinoe. Clary could see it written all over her face. Another boom shook the castle, and dust filtered down from new cracks in the ceiling. The construct holding Melinoe in place was about to come crumbling down around them. If they didn't get out before that happened, Clary feared what would happen to them both. Someone didn't want Melinoe to escape her prison.

A tear trickled out of the goddess's eye. "I can't leave. Every time I try, I end up back here."

"How did you get to me?"

"Sheer will. But I could never escape for long."

"Please trust me, Melinoe. Touch the orb. Hades wouldn't have given it to me if he didn't think it would help you escape."

The goddess closed her eyes and drew in a breath. That alabaster hand reached out again, but touched the orb instead of Clary's face. A shimmer erupted around her. She broke into a million glittery particles that swirled into a stream of silvery light entering the orb.

Clary gazed at the now glowing ball in her hand for a moment, awestruck at what just happened, then shook herself from her trance and stuffed it in the pouch at her waist. She drew her sword and ran back the way she came.

The floor shook as she ran down the stairs. She braced a hand on the wall and kept going. Entering the long hallway, she ran, hoping to find the exit, but it just kept stretching out before her. To her horror, she realized she was now trapped in the same construct holding Melinoe hostage.

"No. No, no, no." She looked out a window. Jumping was not an option. She was four stories up. Movement below caught her eye. A familiar frame paced below. "Colin."

She changed the grip on her sword and used the butt of it to break the glass. He looked up.

"Clary?"

"I'm trapped! There's no exit except the windows."

"Is Ty with you?"

"No. But I have Melinoe in the orb."

"Can you sense Ty at all? Or try to pull him to us? We need him to get you down. He's the only one of us who can fly."

Clary took a deep breath and closed her eyes, focusing on the big man. She searched for his energy, knowing it had to be in the dream-world somewhere. They all drank the same tea, linking them while they slept.

A thread to his psyche glowed in her mind. She reached for it and pulled.

"Holy shit, that was weird."

She opened her eyes to see him standing on the ground next to Colin, arms out to catch his balance. He looked up.

"One moment, I was talking to my parents, the next I was flying through space and landed here."

Clary grimaced. "Sorry. We needed you."

"So I gathered. Somebody catch me up."

"Clary got Melinoe into the orb, but she's trapped up there with no exit. You need to fly up and get her."

"Is that all? Okay." He jumped, shifting into a dragon. Beating his wings, he circled the clearing below before hovering near the window.

"Whoa." She stared at him in wonder. His silvery blue scales shimmered in the strange light like a sunset on water.

The ground shook, and more bits of the castle rained down. A chunk fell off the tower, narrowly missing Colin, who jumped back just in time. Shrieks like they heard earlier split the air. The fog swirled as winged shapes shifted in the clouds.

"Jump, Clary!"

"Right. Yeah." She sheathed her sword, then climbed into the window and braced herself before she pushed off. She landed on Ty's back and flung her arms around his neck and hung on as her momentum tried to carry her over his side.

As soon as she had some semblance of a seat, he swooped toward the ground. The winged creatures they'd only seen shadows of until now emerged from the fog. They were horrific beasts, looking a bit like the demon that answered Hades's door, but uglier. And ten times as scary. Rows and rows of teeth lined their open mouths, visible as they shrieked their displeasure at losing their quarry.

Ty landed on the ground next to Colin, but didn't shift.

"Get on!" Clary motioned him to climb up behind her.

He scrambled onto Ty's back, still moving when Ty took off. Colin reached around her to grab onto Ty's neck as they spiraled into the sky. He let go long enough to lob a fireball at one of the winged beasts that was hot on their tail.

"Babe, get us out of here," he growled.

Clary swallowed her fear and closed her eyes, willing them all to Hades's doorstep. When she opened them, they flew over the path leading to the palace. The front doors opened and Hades stepped out, dressed in full battle gear. Matte black armor cloaked his seven-foot frame. The staff in his hand glowed with fire as he aimed it at them.

"No!" She waved a hand at him. "It's us!"

Ty made a quick turn, then landed at the base of the stairs leading to the door. Clary and Colin climbed down, and he shifted human. As they walked up the steps, all their armor, including Hades's, disappeared.

"Impressive, human." Hades stared at Ty. "How did you know dragons were real?"

Ty snorted. "Because there's a lot scarier shit down here than anything people could think up."

Hades laughed.

Clary pulled out the orb as they reached the top.

His laughter died. "You found her." Eyes locked onto the swirling light, he took a step toward them.

Persephone appeared next to him and pushed past him to take the orb. Tears shimmered in her eyes. "My baby." She looked up at them. "Thank you."

Hades gave them a quick nod. "Yes. Thank you. Follow me." He spun on his heel and entered the palace, Persephone trailing behind him.

Clary looked at Colin and Ty, then shrugged. Ty huffed and followed the gods inside. Colin took her hand, and they stepped forward.

In the foyer, the massive doors closed behind them with a resounding bang. She saw Hades's and Persephone's tall forms hurrying up the massive staircase. They followed. Soon, Clary found herself in the same hallway as before. She tugged on Colin's hand.

"What?" He looked down at her.

"This is where she was. In that other palace."

Hades paused to look back at her. "What did you say?"

Clary's eyes darted between him and her friends before she cleared her throat. "When we found her, she was in this exact place. In a small room at the top of the tower."

The god walked toward her, stopping inches away to stare down at her. "You're sure?"

She nodded. "It's hard to forget a hallway that never ends."

"I assure you, this one ends."

"I hope so. I don't want to be stuck in some loop."

"You're safe here, Clary Moncrief. Always. You rescued my child; a fact that will not be forgotten." He motioned her forward with a nod of his head. "Come. It's time to reunite what was separated."

CHAPTER 29

Creepy didn't begin to describe the feeling Colin got as they walked into the tower room. In the middle of the stone floor on a large four-poster bed laid Melinoe. He knew she wasn't really dead, only in some weird stasis, but she looked dead. Her skin held a sickly pallor, though he wasn't sure that was unusual for her. He remembered reading how she normally looked like the undead. His eyes strayed to the hands crossed over her chest. They looked like wax.

Persephone walked up to the bed and placed the orb on Melinoe's stomach. "Wake, my child."

The light in the orb swirled, excited, before bursting from the glass in a bright shimmer. It hovered above Melinoe for a brief moment before forming into twin streams to enter through her closed eyes.

The goddess's eyes snapped open, glowing silver. She jackknifed as the glow faded, leaving them an eerie amber. In a blink, she was on her feet. Colin edged in front of Clary as the goddess's gaze darted around the room. Anger and a deep wariness turned her mouth down and left her expression hard.

"Melinoe." Persephone's lilting voice broke through her daughter's confusion. She paused, frowning at her mother.

"Mom?"

A relieved smile wreathed Persephone's face. "You're whole, baby. You're safe."

Confusion, a touch of disbelief, and hope replaced Melinoe's hard expression. A tear leaked from her eye. "Mom?" She looked at Hades. "Dad?"

"It's over, Melly," he said.

A sob broke from her, and she collapsed into his open arms. He stroked her two-toned hair, wrapping an arm around his wife and pulling her into their embrace.

Colin glanced at Clary, a bit uncomfortable watching the gods' reunion. It felt like a private moment.

After several moments, they broke apart. Melinoe wiped her face, schooling her emotions. "Can someone tell me what's going on? Why did Phobos and Deimos ambush me?"

"So they were the ones who did this?" Hades growled.

She looked at him and nodded. "I was at home. I went outside to sit in the garden and read. One of them bashed me over the head as I walked out the door. I woke up in the yard with them hovering over me, grinning like maniacal fools. When I asked them what they thought they were doing, they said they were getting what was due to them."

"Due to them?" Hades snorted. "I'll show them what's due them. Bastards. And I'm sure their father will help me."

"We still need to catch them," Ty said.

Melinoe turned, noticing them. Her eyes went to Clary, and she walked over. "Clary Moncrief." In an instant, she yanked Clary from behind Colin's arm to enfold her in a tight hug. "Thank you."

"Um, you're welcome," Clary muttered against the goddess's arm. Melinoe let her go, and Clary stepped back to his side. "Can I ask you something, though?"

"Of course."

"Why me?"

"Because you're the only one who heard me. I searched and searched for anyone who could hear my cries for help. You're the only one who showed up." She took Clary's hands and squeezed them. "Thank you."

Colin looked at Hades. "You need to have a chat with the Fates. This is fucked up."

He snorted. "Agreed. But it is what it is."

"Dad's right. And it's not over. I must get back to Earth and stop the hypnotized from crossing."

"Wait, you know what's going on?" Clary asked.

Melinoe nodded. "Phobos and Deimos are as arrogant as their father. They bragged all about their plan before they gave me some potion they got from Hecate to separate my soul from my body and put me into stasis."

Hades's jaw worked. He shared a look with Persephone. Colin could tell he was planning Hecate's punishment for that fact.

"I think it's time we all got back to Earth," Colin said. "We need to get some real rest for what comes tomorrow."

Hades stepped up next to his daughter and took Clary's hand. "I'm not one to normally appreciate or even thank a human, but I am in your debt." He looked up at Ty and Colin. "All of you."

A grin slashed Ty's face. "Leo will be jealous."

Hades's face soured. "We're not talking about him."

Persephone patted his shoulder. "It's okay, dear." She pulled him back to her side. "Go now and sleep. And thank you for all you've done. We'll meet again one day."

Clary smiled at the goddess.

"Just so long as the next time is after we're dead." Ty arched a brow. "But no promises, right?"

Hades shrugged. "I hope that's the case, but as you said, Colin, the Fates have a fucked up sense of humor. Who knows what they have in store for us?" He smiled and waved a hand at them. "Go. Sleep. And good luck." He turned his gaze to Clary. "And check your pockets when you wake up." He winked.

Before any of them could question what he meant, the world around them faded as the blackness of deep sleep approached.

CHAPTER 30

C lary stretched as she came awake, warm and cozy tucked into Colin's side. As her mind shook off the dregs of sleep, her memory of her dreams the night before came back, and her eyes snapped open. She sat up, clutching the sheet to her naked chest.

Colin yawned and stretched beside her. He stilled as he came fully awake, turning his head to look at her. "We really found her?"

She nodded. "Yeah." A breathy laugh escaped her. "We're one step closer to winning. Now we just need to keep Brandon from hypnotizing everyone and keep Phobos and Deimos from inducing mass panic. Should be a piece of cake." She rolled her eyes and got out of bed, reaching into her suitcase for a pair of underwear. Pulling them up over her hips, she grabbed a bra and shrugged into it, fastening the closure between her breasts.

Clary glanced back to see Colin standing on the other side of the bed, wearing only his boxer briefs as he watched her dress. His aqua eyes were the color of the stormy sea. She chuckled. "After all that happened last night, that's what's on your mind?"

He shrugged and bent over to pick up his jeans, stepping into them. "What can I say? You've got a nice ass."

"The same could be said for you." She yanked a lavender t-shirt over her head, then stepped into her own jeans. When she picked up the sweatshirt to stave off the winter chill, something hard met her hand. Hades's words came back to her. "Colin. There's something in my sweatshirt pocket."

He paused, t-shirt in his hands, and his eyes widened. "Hades said to check your pocket when you woke up."

She nodded and found the opening for the front pocket and slid her hand inside. It closed around a cool, smooth ball. "Why would he—?" She held up the orb.

"What are we supposed to do with that?" He came over to stand next to her.

"I don't know." Clary handed him the orb. "Will it even work for us?"

"I'm not sure." He glanced at the bedside clock. "Everyone should be awake. Let's go find Keira. Maybe she knows. Or Leo. Maybe it gives off some strange vibe only he can see or feel." He handed her back the orb.

After a quick pit stop next door in his room so he could put on a clean shirt, they headed downstairs and found everyone else congregated in the kitchen, eating breakfast.

"About time you two got up. Ty's been filling us in," Leo said.

"Did he tell you about this?" Clary held up the orb.

Ty's eyes went wide. "How did you get that?"

"It was the gift Hades told me to look for in my pocket."

Leo walked over. "May I?"

She handed it to him. "We were hoping you or Keira could tell us what we're supposed to do with it. We don't even know how to use it. Melinoe's soul just touched it and it sucked her in. But she went willingly."

"There's definitely power running through it. I can feel it." He glanced at Keira. "*Chère*, come over here and tell me what you see and feel."

Keira took the orb and closed her eyes as she held it close. "It's a soul stone. Any willing soul can enter the stone, but I think I can force it to accept a non-willing soul with the right potion."

"What good does that do us?" Penny asked.

"I'm not sure. Isolation maybe? It would keep whoever is in it separate from everything else."

A light went off in Clary's head. "Brandon. Even dead, he could hypnotize others. We have to put him in the stone."

Leo grimaced. "I don't like the idea of trapping someone's soul. Even if it is for the greater good. I know how that feels."

A corner of Keira's mouth pulled as she opened her eyes and looked at her husband. "I know. I'm sorry. But that's what it's telling me, and I think Clary's right. Hades probably understands how dangerous he is—dead or alive—and wants to mitigate the threat. He might destroy his soul once he gets the orb back, but this is the safest way to transport him to the underworld."

"Fine." Leo sighed. "But don't ask me to be the one to use it."

Keira shook her head. "No. I think Clary needs to be the one."

"Me?" She looked at the other woman in shock.

"Yes. It's just a feeling, but a strong one." She held the orb out to her.

Clary took it, frowning. "Great." She stuffed it back into her pocket. "So, what's the plan? We're all going to Savannah River, yes?"

"Except Keira and I," Leo said.

"Uh-uh." Keira flicked his bicep. "We're *all* going."

"*Chère*—"

She waved a hand. "I need to be there to make sure that orb works correctly. And you need to be there to fight."

"What about the baby?"

"I think I can help with that," Clary said. A smile quirked her mouth, and she shared a look with Keira.

The other woman grinned, catching on to Clary's plan. "Oh yeah."

"What?" Leo said. "What are you going to do?"

Clary smiled up at him. "Have a conversation."

He frowned. "How?"

She shrugged. "Through dreams. I see the baby's, remember? I'll just make sure he or she understands Keira needs to use her powers if we all want to survive."

"How is an unborn infant supposed to understand that?"

"Because there is nothing normal about your child."

"She has a point, honey." Keira laid a hand on Leo's arm.

He groaned. "Okay, fine. I don't like it, but I think you're all correct. It's going to take all of us to win this."

"Now that we've got that out of the way, Colin, did you talk to that hacker friend of yours about getting a location on Henley's TV broadcast?" Luca said, breaking into the conversation.

"Yes. She said she'd call once she was in and had something to report."

"Will that be soon, do you think?"

He lifted a shoulder. "Maybe. She's pretty good."

"In the meantime," Leo said, "we should get on the road. We're running out of time."

Clary agreed. She didn't want to leave this until the last minute. They were cutting it close as it was. The longer they waited, the further Brandon and his godly cohorts got in their plan, and the harder they became to stop. Losing wasn't an option.

CHAPTER 31

"Is she sure this is the place?" Luca asked, staring up at the mundane office building in Augusta, Georgia Charisse's intel led them to.

Colin nodded. "This is the address she found."

Ty put down the night-vision binoculars he was using. "Well, it looks empty, so I think we probably have the right place." He pointed to the roof. "That satellite dish didn't get there by itself."

"Nope. And it's hooked up. I can see the electricity it's using." Leo opened his car door and got out. "It's not transmitting yet, though." He looked at his watch. "We don't have much time. It'll be midnight overseas in an hour."

"What happened to we weren't going to cut this so close?" Clary asked, coming around the other side of the car.

Colin shut his door with a soft click. "Henley's hacker is better than we thought he'd be. It took Charisse longer to find him."

"It doesn't matter," Keira said, getting out the other side. "We're here now. Let's do this."

"Where are all the guards?" Luca asked as they moved toward the building. "Shouldn't there be guards?"

"If I was the one doing this, I would keep the guards inside out of public view," Leo said. "Everyone, hang back a moment. I'm going to check things out and find us a way in." Before anyone could respond, he took off.

Ty rolled his eyes. "Keep moving. By the time we get close enough to need to know where we're headed, he'll be back."

"One day, he'll get used to the fact that things take less time now," Keira said.

In pairs, they moved forward, keeping to the shadows. Colin cracked the door on his ability to control the darkness, making sure the shadows followed them. They reached the edge of the property when Leo reappeared.

"I told you guys to stay put."

"We're being proactive." Ty gestured to the building. "What did you find?"

"There's a way in on the far side. I also went inside and found their central hub. We won't all reach it together without a distraction."

Ty grinned and looked at Penny. "You up for some prowling, babe?"

She scrunched her face. "I guess. Cats?"

He nodded. "Sure. They're quick. But maybe smaller than a mountain lion, since we'll be indoors."

Leo held up a hand. "Let's get inside before you shift." He motioned them around the building.

Colin kept the darkness close, conscious of the cameras mounted on the roof. Leo stopped at a side door. He cracked it open and peered inside.

"They just left it open?" Clary asked.

Leo looked back with a grin. "Not exactly." He motioned to the door with a quick nod of his head. "Come on."

They filed inside. Colin was thankful for the dark. It made his job of keeping them concealed easier. He couldn't muffle their footsteps, though, so they tread lightly down the hall with Leo leading the way. At the end of the corridor, they paused.

"Past there is where the guards are." Leo pointed at Ty and Penny. "You two distract them. The rest of us will get into the room where Henley is holed up."

"Did you see Phobos or Deimos?" Luca asked.

He shook his head. "That doesn't mean they aren't close, so keep your eyes open." He looked at Ty and Penny. "You ready?"

They looked at each other and nodded.

Leo opened the door. In a single movement, they shifted and leaped through. Colin heard shouts of surprise, then screams of terror as Ty and Penny attacked. Gunfire sounded, and his heart leaped into his throat. He sent up a fervent prayer that none of the bullets connected with his friends.

Shouts and the tread of running footsteps came from the adjacent hallways.

"That's a lot of feet," Colin whispered.

"Blind them." Leo ran through the door.

"Blind—shit!" Colin closed his eyes and threw open the door to the darkness, creating pockets around his friends. Wild bursts of gunfire erupted beyond the door, accompanied by more screams, until it all suddenly went quiet.

"Do you think it's safe now?" Clary asked.

Colin opened his eyes, but kept the darkness in place. Flames erupted in his hands. "Get behind me." He stepped inside, ready to set fire to anyone in his path.

"We're good, Col." Ty shifted human near a bank of computers across the room. "And I don't ever want to hear how freaky it is to see me glow blue again. Your eyes are roiling with flames and you're holding fireballs."

"Good to know." He released his hold on the flames and the darkness. Dim light lit the room.

Keira gasped. "Dear God."

Dear God was right. Blood splattered the walls and floor, even the ceiling. Chairs lay toppled in front of the desks. Colin counted ten bodies on the floor.

"How are we going to explain this to the police?" she asked.

"We're not," Leo said. "Once we catch Phobos and Deimos—and they will be here to witness the broadcast if they're as arrogant as I think they are—I'm sure Hades will be perfectly willing to send another cleanup crew."

"He burned the bodies last time, remember?" Keira shot back.

"None of that matters," Colin interrupted. They had bigger things to worry about first. He zeroed in on the man cowering in the corner and stalked over to him, lifting him to his feet by his shirt. "Where are your friends? And all the bombs you built?"

A victorious smile lifted one corner of Henley's mouth. "You'll never stop them all, detective." He looked past Colin. "Hello, Clary. I'd be lying if I said I hoped you wouldn't show up. I always wanted you by my side in this, but you refused to be coerced."

Colin's brows dipped as Henley's words registered. He shook the smaller man. "What? What do you mean?"

"Did you try to hypnotize me?" Clary stepped up to Colin's side.

"I didn't think anyone could resist me. You not only did, you didn't even realize I was trying. It was like there was a barrier in your mind I couldn't breach. Tell me how that's possible."

"You bastard," she said through clenched teeth. "I trusted you. You perverted everything we worked on. Everything I thought we stood for."

"No. It's what you stood for. I never had the same agenda. Humans are a blight on this world."

"So you thought you could eradicate us all—except yourself, of course," Colin said.

"I'm needed. To keep those who survive in line."

Ty scoffed. "Is that the line those gods fed you? Once you've outlived your usefulness, they'll kill you."

His mouth quirked again. "Only if I can't persuade them otherwise. It's worked well for me so far."

"Because we let it."

Dread filled Colin. He turned at the sound of the unfamiliar voice to see one of the twins in the doorway. Judging by how he felt, he'd hazard a guess it was Deimos. An evil smile spread over the god's face as he stepped into the room.

"My, you have been busy. My father should recruit you all. I thought Dr. Henley hired the best to protect him and our hacker."

"Ungifted humans are no match for our kind," Leo said. "You should have known that and insisted he hire others like us. I'm sure there are plenty in the mercenary ranks."

"Yes, but they're busy with other tasks." His smile grew.

Likely preparing to lead armies, Colin thought. Or setting the bombs they still needed to find. He took a deep breath, compartmentalizing the dread Deimos induced, and took one hand off Henley to let the flames light again. "Nice haircut." He nodded at the shortened length where the god cut off the singed ends from their previous encounter. "I can make it shorter, if you want."

The smile on Deimos's face died. "I will enjoy sending you to see my uncle."

From the corner of his eye, Colin saw Keira edge behind Henley. He knew she had the orb, but it would take time to trap Henley's soul. They needed to keep Deimos busy and his focus elsewhere.

"Where's your brother?"

"He'll be along soon. Can't you feel the fear? I have to admit, you all are better at conquering it than most. But there's more at stake this time. More to fear." His eyes landed on Keira. "Tell me, witch—how big of a blast can you contain?"

The dread burst free of its box. He cast a glance at Ty and could tell he was having the same thought. There was a bomb in the building.

They shared a look with the others. Leo's eyes went silver a split second before he moved.

"Now!" Colin threw up a wall of fire between them and the fight behind him.

Henley's eyes widened and his mouth opened on a silent shout of surprise as Colin sent fire through his heart at the same time Clary pressed the orb to the back of his neck and Keira muttered a spell. Light burst from Brandon's eyes to form into a chaotic ball over his head. It swirled angrily before streaming into the orb. His body went limp in Colin's grasp. He let the man drop to the floor, then spun to see if Leo needed help.

The flame curtain dropped to reveal the two gods grappling with each other, reappearing in brief flashes in different places throughout the room as they fought. Colin tried to gauge an opening, but they simply moved too fast. Leo was on his own for now.

Fear sucker punched him in the gut. It loosed the dread he'd kept at bay, weighing down his muscles even as it sent his heart rate into overdrive. He pulled on every ounce of self-control he possessed and pushed back the panic that wanted him to run from the room. A whoosh of air was the only herald before Phobos appeared in the doorway. He took in the fight, then the others standing watch in an instant. A slow smile spread over his face. In what felt like slow motion, he moved toward Keira, pulsing fear at them all.

Leo's focus faltered and Deimos landed a blow that sent him across the room. He smashed into the wall of monitors, sending them crashing down to the floor.

Colin spun around, intending to step in front of Keira, but Luca beat him to it. As he dove in front of her, he pulled water from the sprinkler system and turned the droplets into razor thin slivers and sent them toward Phobos.

But even as they moved through the god's body like hundreds of tiny knives, his momentum carried him toward Luca. He barreled into him at speed, sending them both sailing into the wall. Plaster and ceiling tiles rained down as the force of the impact shook the room and the wall crumbled, leaving behind the steel structure behind it.

Everyone, including Deimos, paused before the room descended into complete chaos. Having recovered from crashing into the computer bank, Leo shot across the room to stand in front of Keira. Eyes glowing silver, he faced Deimos. Colin unleashed the darkness again, blinding the god, but being the warrior he was, he used his other senses to locate them. He lashed out, landing a blow to Ty's chin.

Ty staggered back, falling into the desk, before sliding to the floor. Penny jumped on Deimos's back, shifting into an octopus, using her tentacles to trap his arms to his sides. Colin let go of the darkness to focus his efforts on his other abilities. His hands erupted with flames. He raised them, preparing to send a stream of fire at the god's heart. It was time to end this.

The building shook as the first stream left his hand.

"What was that?" Ty stood.

They all paused as it continued to shake. Dread permeated the room, but it wasn't directed at any of them. Colin got the distinct feeling it was what Deimos felt. Moments later, the ceiling crashed down, the framework for the drop ceiling falling down around them. Colin ducked, covering his head, then looked up as the dust settled.

In the middle of the wreckage rose a man, imposing and frightening in his intensity. Colin's eyes widened as he took in the newcomer. He bore a resemblance to Hades and Ty, but lacked Hades's kingly manner and Ty's heroic countenance.

Deimos groaned and struggled against Penny's hold. "What are you doing here?"

The newcomer walked forward and, instead of speaking to Deimos, looked Penny in the eye. "Release him."

Ty stepped forward, but the man held out a hand. "I mean her no harm."

Penny unwound her tentacles and shifted human, climbing off Deimos. Leo stepped forward.

"Who are you?"

The man spared Leo a quick glance. "His father."

Colin sucked in a sharp breath and looked around at the others. They all wore identical expressions. Why was Ares here?

"Go home, Dad."

"I will. With you and your brother." He glanced back at Phobos, who still lay unconscious on the floor with Luca. He grimaced. "Though I should let these humans finish you off. You're a disgrace. What were you thinking?"

"A disgrace? You're the disgrace. When was the last time you conquered anyone? When we ruled on the battlefield and man feared us?"

"They don't need to fear us. And we fight when we're needed. This fight was not necessary. Hecate wants to end us all and you let her convince you she'd let you live. Father's ready to turn you over to Hades and let him send you to the pits of Tartarus for what you did to Melinoe. I convinced him to let me deal with you. You're lucky that one found your cousin's soul, or there would be nothing I could do to stop him." He pointed at Clary.

A look of surprise crossed Deimos's face, and he looked at Clary. "You found Melinoe?"

She nodded, but said nothing.

He cursed, and his shoulders fell.

"Your plans are ruined." Ares held up an orb similar to the one Keira possessed, except it was gold. "Give me your powers."

"What?" Deimos's eyes widened.

"Until we can be sure you'll use them as intended, Father demanded they be under my purview. Touch the orb, Deimos."

Deimos crossed his arms, defiance flashing on his face. "No."

In a blink, Ares had his son by the throat, feet dangling inches above the floor. "I'm not asking. Don't make me use the witch to take them."

Keira squawked and curled her fingers into Leo's shirt. Deimos's eyes bounced from his father to her and back again. He struggled to nod in Ares's hold, defeat now in the lines of his body. Ares lowered him to the floor. With one finger, Deimos touched the orb in his father's hand. Silver light streamed from him into the orb, making it glow for a moment before it sank into the sphere.

Ares nodded once, then took a fistful of his son's shirt. He pocketed the orb, then walked over to Phobos and picked him up by his waistband. Phobos's back bowed, his arms hanging limp to trail on the ground. Blood trickled from his wounds to drip onto the floor. Ares turned to look at them all. "Thank you for trying to stop them. I assure you, they won't be a problem again. And I'm sorry about your friend." He nodded once at Luca's prone form, then as quickly as he arrived, he disappeared through the hole in the ceiling in one powerful leap.

Colin stared up after him for a long moment before his words registered. "Wait. Sorry about—" Alarmed, he hurried to Luca's side, dropping to his knees to check for a pulse. Nothing, not even a flicker, met his fingers.

He looked up at the others. "He's dead."

CHAPTER 32

C lary pushed back the tears that wanted to fall as she looked down at Luca's body. It wouldn't help their situation for her to fall apart now. Colin wrapped his hands over her shoulders and turned her away.

"Do we still think there's a bomb in the building?" Ty asked, looking at his partner.

"I wouldn't doubt it. Whether it's nuclear or not, we're close enough to Savannah River to draw attention away from the site and make it easier for them to initiate a meltdown," Colin replied. "I also think we need to split up."

"And go where?" Ty said. "Savannah River?"

Colin nodded. "Clary might be the only one who can stop them." He looked at her. "Unless you think their hypnosis ended with Henley's death."

She frowned. "I suppose it's possible, but we need to make sure."

"All right. You and I can go there. The rest of you, find the bomb here."

"Wait." Ty held out a hand. "Your skills would be more useful here. You're better at defusing explosives. Let Keira go with Clary. Leo, you go too."

"I have a better idea," Clary said. "It will be too difficult for all three of us to get past security at the nuclear facility. Leo, you go, and bring back the manager. If anyone would be hypnotized, it would be the man in charge. While you're gone, the rest of us can search here for the bomb. We need to get a line on the others around the world too. This is far from over."

Leo nodded. "That's a good plan. I'll be right back." He took off in a blur.

"Everyone split up," Colin said. "Take a floor. I'll start in the basement, because that's where I'd put a bomb if I wanted to bring the whole building down."

They scattered, running out the door to the stairwell. Colin went down while the others went up.

CHAPTER 33

Gun drawn just to be safe, Colin reached for the light switch as he exited the stairs. He flipped the switches, but nothing happened. Emergency lights cast a dim glow from their positions near the ceiling. He frowned. Ares's entrance must have knocked out the building's power. He flipped on the flashlight attached to his weapon and advanced.

As a bomb tech, Colin had been in many buildings like this one, both for training and in real-world scenarios. He went to the most structural points, checking them one by one. It didn't take him long to find the device.

He dropped to his knees in front of the bomb, which was strapped to a support column. A green light blinked back at him with steady flashes. Red numbers ticked down from ten minutes, twenty-two seconds.

"I found the device," he said, pressing the button on his throat mic to activate it. "Keep looking for other bombs." He let go and turned all his focus to the mess of wires and C-4 in front of him. This one was similar to the one on Henley's boat. Just bigger. He traced the wires, locating the one leading to the detonator. He wrapped his fingers around it to pull it, but the glint of copper from behind the timer caught his attention just before he did. He froze, then let go to lean in and look closer. Something was contacting the wire's post.

A curse slid past his lips as he realized the wire was a dummy trigger. If he pulled it, it wouldn't stop the device. The real trigger was behind the timer. He pressed his mic button again. "I need some help down here."

Leo appeared at his side in an instant.

"I thought you were at Savannah River?"

"I was. They were in damage control mode. Seems Henley's influence stopped with his death. I left them to it. What do you need from me?"

"Hold the light. I need two hands." He handed Leo his gun.

"It feels very strange to be pointing a loaded weapon at a bomb." Leo held the light on the timer.

Colin's mouth quirked. "All of this feels strange." He dug in his pocket and withdrew a multi-tool and quickly unscrewed the faceplate. Carefully, so as not to jar the wires underneath, he pulled the plastic away to look behind it.

"Damn. This is what I was hoping it wasn't."

"What?"

"It's a redundant switch. If either end loses contact or we break the circuit, it explodes."

"So, how do we stop it?"

Colin's mouth turned down, and he glanced at Leo. "We don't."

"What? No, there has to be a way. Colin, if this goes off, a lot of people will die. There are apartments on either side of this building."

Blowing out a breath, he swiped a hand down his face. "If I could patch in a different timer, I could fool it into giving us more time. We could evacuate the buildings, then."

Leo frowned. "I'd rather not let anyone else in on this."

"Newsflash, there's a giant hole in the middle of the building, and the ground shook like mad just a little while ago. I'd be shocked if the cops aren't already on their way."

"Because, of course, this can't be simple. Okay. Can you bypass the timer?"

Colin was already pulling his phone out to take the back off. "Yep." He glanced around. "I need some wire. Anything copper."

Leo found a desk and laid the gun down, pointing the light his way, then punched a wall and pulled out the wiring, breaking off a section.

With a couple of quick movements, Colin stripped the insulation off the wire, then attached one end to his phone's wiring. He turned it over and opened his timer app, setting it for the maximum time it would let him. "Hold this." He handed it to Leo. Taking the other end of the wire, he slid it between the post and the wire going to the bomb's timer and prayed.

When nothing happened, he disconnected the timer from its power source. His phone now controlled the bomb.

"Can we just pause the timer?" Leo asked.

"Maybe. Let me double check a few things." He went back over the device, wire by wire, connection by connection. Nothing indicated it would go off if they stopped the timer. He looked at Leo. "Do it."

"Okay. Here it goes." Leo inhaled a breath and held it. He pressed pause.

Colin braced himself.

"Are we still alive?"

"I don't feel dead. And you'd think we'd wake up somewhere besides here."

"True. Now what?"

"Now I disconnect everything." He reached for the first wire.

Sirens echoed from outside.

"Damn." He glanced at the door. "We're running out of time."

"Disconnect it all. I'll get the bodies out of here."

Colin blinked, and he was gone. He shook his head. "One day, I'll get used to that."

Working quickly, he dismantled the bomb, finding a bucket in the janitor's closet and loading it up. As he put the last piece in, Leo reappeared.

"Time to go."

"Take that." Colin pointed to the bucket. "I'll meet you outside."

"Go out the back." Leo vanished.

Colin rocketed up the stairs, running into the others as they made their way out of the building.

"Keira, make a bubble," Ty said. "We don't want the first responders to see us."

She nodded. The hair on the back of Colin's neck rose as energy coalesced around them. They reached the door, but Colin skidded to a stop. "Wait."

"What? Col, we need to leave," Ty said.

"I know. But we're leaving a lot of evidence behind. Things that could point back to us."

"It can't be helped."

Colin looked down at his hands. "It can." He took a few steps back. "You go. I'll catch up." He spun around and ran back toward the computer room, ignoring their protests.

He wove through the halls until he reached the room. Standing in the middle, he glanced around. Blood stained the floor and walls, not all of it belonging to the bad guys. He paused when his gaze landed on Luca. Remorse made his heart ache. He wished he could take the man from here, but knew he needed to stay. There was no other way to explain his injuries and death.

Looking away, he saw that Leo also left Henley, tying up the story of what happened here. Well, all except the giant hole in the ceiling. He looked up and shook his head. No cop or firefighter in their right mind would believe a fire caused that hole. He hoped Leo left some of that C-4 behind to explain this.

He didn't have time to look, though. It was time to erase their presence. His hands ignited. He sent streaks of flames around the room, lighting every surface on fire. By the time he had it burning well, he could hear voices and footfalls coming his way. There was no way he could leave the way he came. His eyes went to the hole above him again. He glanced down at his hands, an idea forming.

"This better work." He let the fire burn brighter. "I always wondered what it would be like to be Ironman. Guess it's time to find out." He blasted fire at the ground, lifting himself. Concentrating, he lit his feet, adding to the force. He heard the first responders getting closer and knew he needed to move faster. Praying he didn't burn himself up, he let the flames take hold and shot toward the sky in a ball of flames. He rocketed through the roof, looking like a flashover to anyone on the ground, and went over the side of the building, out of sight of the street.

As he looked for a place to land, Clary's blonde hair stood out to him like a beacon. She glanced up as he came down.

"You okay?" He asked, touching down beside her.

She stared at him, open-mouthed. "Did you—how did you—?"

"Dude." Ty ran up. "How are you not burned?"

He shrugged. "It's my fire. Come on. I know Keira's shielding us, but you never know who might show up." He took Clary's hand and led her away from the building.

"What did you guys do with the bodies?" Colin asked as he they reached the car. He opened the door and ushered Clary inside, then followed her.

"I left them in a marsh. The gators will erase any trace of them."

"What about the other bombs? What are we doing about them?"

"Call Charisse," Leo said. "Have her track the last signal from that building. I'll do the same once we get back to the estate. Once we find them, we can contact the authorities anonymously and have them go in to disarm the devices. I think it's the best we can hope for in the time we have left. Hopefully, none of them go off first."

Colin nodded, and reached for his phone, remembering as his hand hit his empty pocket that he used it to disarm the bomb. "Um, can I borrow someone's phone?"

Leo chuckled and handed his over.

He took it and dialed Charisse's number. When she picked up, he asked her to do as Leo said, but also asked her to use her encrypted phone line to inform the authorities of the bombs. They didn't need any of this tracing back to them.

"There. That's done." He handed Leo back his phone. "The authorities should be here soon. We should probably scoot. I don't like leaving Luca behind, but we don't want to be tangled up in this."

"I agree. You want to Ironman us out of here?" Ty's mouth lifted.

Colin rolled his eyes. "Very funny."

EPILOGUE

Soft sand filtered between Clary's fingers as she ran her hands through the fine grains. Waves lapped just feet away. She never wanted to leave this spot. She'd always loved the beach, but Greek beaches were something else. So was the water. She'd never seen water so blue. They might be in Greece to talk to the Oracle, but she wasn't going to pass up the opportunity for some beach time.

As she stared over the sea, enjoying the breeze, Colin rose from the waves. Water sluiced from his muscled frame, highlighting his toned body and making his tattoos stand out in sharp relief. Clary's mouth turned as dry as the sand as she watched him walk toward her. He swept his hair back and smiled.

"Hey. When did you get down here?"

"A little while ago. Ty told me you went for a swim, so I decided to come find you."

He sank into the sand beside her and gave her a kiss. "I'm glad. Alone time together has been a rare thing this week."

"No kidding. So has sleep. You'd think Keira could find something to help her calm that baby." Keira and Leo's newborn son, Remy, was giving them all fits with his colicky tummy. They'd tried to make this trip months ago, before Keira delivered, but complications with her pregnancy kept her from flying.

"Leo said she tried, but he seems to be immune to anything she does."

"Hmm. Maybe I should try getting into one of his dreams. See if I can't find out what would help."

He leaned in, nuzzling her neck. "Might be worth a shot. Then we wouldn't have to spend all the night-time hours sleeping when we can. There are other things that could occupy our time."

She chuckled and pushed him back. "As much as I would love to get sand in all the wrong places, we don't have time. We're supposed to head out soon, remember?"

He sighed, then nipped her shoulder and sat back, propping an arm over his bent knee. "Yeah. I remember."

"Don't look so glum." She got to her feet and held out her hands. "We've got another week of vacation left. I promise there will be more beach time before we go back to the U.S."

He took her hands and rose, using their hold to tug her in close. "I'll hold you to that."

Pressing a kiss to her lips, he let his hands roam down her body. Clary wished she'd donned her swimsuit before she came down instead of staying in her t-shirt and shorts. She wanted to feel his hands on her.

The last seven months together had been nothing short of amazing. After the authorities rounded up all the players involved in Henley's plan, life returned to normal with just a few changes. Colin's friend, Charisse, was able to plant files on Henley's computer tying him to the attempted bombings, and Leo broke into the FBI headquarters to plant files in Luca's office showing he was on Henley's trail when he was killed. It was all tied up with a nice, pretty bow. Once they were sure no one was looking at them, Clary found a new research partner. One Colin vetted thoroughly before she committed to working with her. They also moved in together. They ended up in the same dream almost every night, anyway. It felt weird to wake up alone after sharing such intimacy.

Voices coming down the staircase built into the cliff face drew their attention. They looked over to see their friends on their way down.

"We must have lingered longer than I thought," Colin said. "I guess it's time to go. I hope one of them brought me a change of clothes."

Clary laughed. "From what I've read about the Oracle, she probably won't mind if you show up the way you are."

He grinned. "Yes, well, there's only one woman I want getting excited about seeing me undressed." His eyes heated.

Clary's body hummed, but she slapped a lid on it.

The others stepped off the staircase and headed for the dock. Ty whistled and motioned for Colin and Clary to join them.

As they walked closer, Leo ran an assessing eye over them and sighed. He handed the baby carrier to Keira. "I'll be right back." In a blink, he was gone, only to return a moment later with some of Colin's clothes.

"Thanks." Colin took the items and followed his friends on board the boat. While he retreated to a bedroom to dress, Clary followed Keira and Penny into the living quarters while Ty and Leo went to the wheelhouse to cast the boat off. After they made their way to Skiathos, they would catch a plane to take them to mainland Greece. It was a long day of traveling, but they all hoped it would be worth it. If the Fates had anything else in store for them, they wanted to know.

***

The sun was setting as they pulled into a small roadside parking lot at Delphi. Clary got out of the van and stretched. "So, this is the spot?" She glanced up the hill. Ruins were all that met her gaze. "It doesn't look like much."

"That's because these ruins were just the temple above Pythia's home."

They all whirled at the new voice intruding. Persephone stood at the edge of the trees on the other side of the car.

She smiled at them and tipped her head. "It's this way."

They followed her into the trees and down into a gully. At the bottom, a cave opened into the side of the mountain.

"I'm glad it's you showing us the way and not Hades." Leo looked around, a wary expression on his handsome face. "I'd be worried he was leading us to our doom, otherwise."

Persephone laughed. "He still grumbles about you."

"Yeah? Well, it's mutual, trust me."

"How are things down there?" Clary asked. "How's Melinoe?" Since they stopped Henley, Phobos, and Deimos, and rescued Melinoe's soul, she hadn't been able to stop thinking about the goddess.

"She's doing well. Zeus didn't let Phobos and Deimos squeak by, or let Ares handle the punishment. He let Hades take them. They're rotting beside Hecate."

"You sure that's wise? Letting them talk?" Ty asked.

"Oh, they're not together. I just meant they're in the same place. They have their own separate hells to deal with."

"Good." Colin nodded once. "After all they did, they deserve it."

"I agree." She stopped at a metal door built into the wall. "This is it." Grasping the handle, she pulled.

"It's not locked?" Leo asked.

"Only those who are meant to see it, see it."

"How does she know who's meant to see it?" Clary glanced around at the smooth rock walls as Persephone led them into the mountain. Thick carpet silenced their footfalls. Ornate lighting and million-dollar paintings decorated the space.

Persephone shrugged. "She's the Oracle."

Ty snorted. "You know, I don't think Zeus is the one really in charge. I think it's Pythia."

Persephone smiled. "I would have to agree. But don't tell him that."

"Tell who what?" A woman in a deep red silk dress with her dark hair drawn into a sleek braid walked out of a room and smiled at them.

"How you have Zeus wrapped around your little finger and always have." Persephone grinned.

"Ah, yes. But you all didn't come here to discuss my relationship with our fearless leader." She motioned them toward the room she just exited. "Come."

Clary's eyes widened as she turned into the room. Modern opulence oozed from every corner. Being the Oracle must pay well.

"Sit, please." She gestured to the couches clustered around a live edge coffee table.

Wary, the group sat, watching the goddess as they did so. Clary folded her hands in her lap to keep from fidgeting. What Pythia said in the next few minutes could change a lot of things.

"So, you're the band of humans who saved us all. Thank you. And I see you've added to your group." She tipped her head to the sleeping baby strapped to Keira's chest.

"Yes." Keira laid a protective hand over her son's back. "We wanted to come before he was born, but complications kept us in the U.S."

Pythia nodded. "I'm aware. Your next pregnancy will be much easier."

"Next?" Keira frowned. "You can see that? And why are you being so clear about it? Don't you normally talk in riddles?"

The goddess laughed, the sound tinkling merrily through the room. "Not always, no. And yes. I see much about all of you."

"Such as?" Leo asked.

"Family. Love. Lives well-lived."

"So, does that mean we're done being Hades's special forces?" Ty asked.

She shook her head. "No. All it means is when you're not fighting to save the world, you will be happy."

"We'd be happier being left alone," Leo growled.

Pythia's smile was soft and contained a touch of sorrow. "I know. But you weren't given your gifts so you could be a normal person. The world needs you. It needs all of you."

His mouth pulled, but he said nothing.

"So, how does this work?" Colin asked. "Is Hades just going to keep popping up, expecting us to drop everything? That's not going to work. We have jobs. Families." He gestured to Keira and Leo.

"Agreed. Which is why I spoke to Hades, Zeus, and Poseidon and proposed an alliance of sorts. Persephone, would you like to explain?"

"We realize us showing up the way we have is disruptive," Persephone started. "And that it can be difficult for you to explain your presence and involvement to human authorities. We want to bankroll an organization devoted to supernatural occurrences. One run and staffed by you and others like you."

"So, what? We're like supernatural bounty hunters?" Penny said.

"In a sense, I suppose. Hades and I like to think of you more as gatekeepers. You're the last line of defense before our worlds collide."

"Shouldn't all of this be done, though?" Keira said. "Or does Hecate have a backup for her backup?" She looked at Pythia.

"It's not just Hecate," the goddess replied. "The walls between the worlds are blurred now. Too much has happened, and they've started to crumble. We need you on this side of things to keep them from falling down. The hope is to eventually shore them up, but it will take time. Time we don't have without you."

"What happens if we say no?" Colin asked.

"You won't."

Colin narrowed his eyes at her. "Humor me. What would happen?"

She sighed. "That happiness I mentioned—it wouldn't last long. If the divide falls, the world as you know it disappears with it."

Clary and the others shared looks. It sounded like their new normal was taking a turn.

"Okay," Leo said. "How does this work? Are we independent, or do we report to someone?"

"Hades and his brothers have established a reporting chain for our side. Anything unusual noted by the gods will get sent up the chain to Hermes," Persephone said. "He can travel between Olympus and the underworld, which makes him ideal for the post. The most serious threats he will take to one of the brothers, who will decide if it warrants your intervention."

"What if we note something strange, but aren't sure it's worthy of our attention?" Ty asked.

"You'll route it to Hermes, just like we do."

"How?"

Persephone pointed at Keira.

"Me?"

"Yes. You're the conduit."

"Lovely."

"Don't worry. You'll have help," Pythia said. "Eventually, anyway. Your daughter will inherit your abilities."

Leo growled. "Those are things humans like to learn on their own."

She had the good grace to look chagrined. "Sorry. I meant no harm. I deal in information and I forget that not everyone wants to know what I know."

He blew out a breath. "I think we all will have a learning curve over the next few months." He glanced around at the others. "So, are we doing this?"

"I vote yes," Ty said. "We've seen what's on the other side. It needs to stay there."

"I agree," Penny said.

"Same," Clary said. She had no desire to unleash hell on Earth.

"I vote yes, too," Colin said.

All eyes turned to Keira. She held up her hands. "My vote was yes the moment she said the wall was coming down. I don't want my children growing up during the apocalypse."

Leo ran his hands over his face. "Fine. We're in."

Afterword

Thank you for reading *The Dreamcatcher*! I hope you enjoyed it. Please consider leaving a rating or review. It would be greatly appreciated!